Misbegotten

James Gabriel Berman is the author of *Uninvited*, which was nominated for an Edgar Award and translated into over ten languages. He lives in Boston where he is working on a new novel.

James Gabriel Berman
Misbegotten

FOURTH ESTATE · London

First published in Great Britain in 1996 by
Fourth Estate Limited
6 Salem Road
London W2 4BU

Copyright © 1996 by James Gabriel Berman

The right of James Gabriel Berman to be identified as the author of this work has been asserted by him in accordance with the Copyright, Designs and Patents Act 1988.

A catalogue record for this book is available from the British Library.

ISBN 1 85702 444 3 (Pbk)
ISBN 1 85702 584 9 (Hbk)

All rights reserved. No part of this publication may be reproduced, transmitted, stored in a retrieval system, in any form or by any means, without permission in writing from Fourth Estate Limited.

Typeset by CentraCet Ltd, Cambridge
Printed in Great Britain by
Clays Ltd, St Ives plc, Bungay, Suffolk

A child arrived just the other day,
He came to the world in the usual way.
— Harry Chapin, from 'Cat's in the Cradle', by Sandy & Harry Chapin

MISBEGOTTEN

1

Appliances are bad company.

And so, for Caitlin Bourke, the third snow of winter brought a longing for the sun, for skin that didn't dry like parchment. And for a baby.

In the kitchen, the only sound was the refrigerator hum – so useless in this weather: she could keep the milk on the expansive deck outside the bedroom, the eggs on the front sloping lawn, the butter and cheese on the hood of the Range Rover parked on the gravel drive outside. In the suburbs of Westbridge, when it's cold and there's no place to go, appliances are bad company.

As it blizzarded and the crisp cold shut off the sounds of life so that the only thing notable on all of the six acres of the Bourke homestead was the stirring of trees sloughing off their winter burden, the need for a child assaulted her. She knew she wanted this baby so selfishly. Not with any of the tender, fleshy maternity with which her mother had wanted her, but instead with a disabling need, a desperation for another being to fill the dreary space of those many rooms.

Caitlin wondered what it would be like. To step from kitchen to living room knowing there was one more room occupied, one more voice, one more spirit. That was what she wanted. One more spirit so that she wouldn't have to continue the endless listening to her own.

In the living room on the mantel was a picture of her husband. A tall, silent, sandy-haired man with big hands which he liked to clasp behind his back when listening to you, Paul Bourke was the type that didn't speak until spoken to. An excellent quality in a husband, according to many wives in Westbridge. Yet he lacked a characteristic that most of them required, and one that most husbands provided in due biological course: the ability to squire the next generation.

He blamed it on toxins – on waste dumps, nuclear power plants, high-voltage electric generators, and lead paint.

Paul had never been an environmentalist until the doctor told them he couldn't have a child. After the news, he had taken early retirement from his job as Vice-President of a petrochemical company and gone into business for himself – an environmentalist venture – looking for ways to harness solar energy in satellites. If he couldn't father a child, Caitlin figured, he would father a company. And that he did, with tremendous success.

She remembered the day in the doctor's office. She had taken a Valium that morning because she knew it would be the day that they would find out who was responsible. She wanted it to be her: *If it can be me, then let it be, because I can take responsibility for it in a way Paul never will, and God knows I want to take responsibility for it. God knows I do because then I'll know that I never could have married the right man.* But when the doctor met them in the consultation room, Caitlin knew. The doctor began slowly, with an all too professional tenor, in a way that meant it was bad news. And if it was bad news, it had to be Paul, because a male doctor would think that, by definition, to be the worst news of all.

MISBEGOTTEN

She'd dreamed of giving birth many times. She'd imagined the usefulness of it. She had forever been useless herself. But the usefulness of a new being. It was undeniable. She'd imagined her new child sliding out of her legs effortlessly. The pain never appeared in the dreams. The genderless child always emerged, fully dressed, fully schooled, and talking to her as no one had ever talked to her before.

From the living room, she passed to the den. It was humble, book-lined on two walls, cosy, and filled with the mustiness of the winter's seclusion. This was her favourite room. All the many others were sterile – she could not imagine life growing there. But here in the den – this was where she imagined herself nursing. On the plump sofa that was more comfortable than any bed could be, she watched herself, breast bared, satisfying the largest of small cravings. Of course, one of the rooms upstairs would be for the crib and baby furnishings and the muted shades of whatever colour wallpaper would be appropriate. And that would be where the toys would accumulate, in rapid succession, with each month and then birthday and then occasion. She had not picked out the exact room yet. It would be either on the left or right off the head of the stairs and picking which one was like picking a boy or a girl – something you could not do.

Caitlin sat on the couch and listened to the house. So much of a house was what it sounded like, she thought. That was something you never could detect when you came first with the brokers. With all the talk of down-payments, septic systems, taxes, structural integrity and zoning rules, there was no way to hear the sounds of the house. This house had the brooding silence that could cause discomfort in even small doses, yet when compounded over time could probe deeper and deeper and ulcerate the toughest of constitutions.

In the kitchen the refrigerator hummed, content to feed on the electricity that flowed effortlessly through a hundred outlets, down from the wires outside, through the cold, wintry landscape, from the generator eighteen miles south of Kingsbridge. The humming was in chorus with the silence. And the silence was in chorus with the light snowfall that, with gradual insistence, buried Paul's morning footprints on the front steps.

2

In Northport, there's no money.

Billy Crapshoot didn't mind. He would find some, somewhere. The usual way perhaps, with a gun to someone's neck, in their car, when they were coming home from work, and were stopped at a traffic light, near the train station maybe, preferably on the end of Morone Street, where there's no storefront not empty, and the sun sets early in winter. It was easy to get money this way. Like this: wait at the light, well dressed, act refined. Spot the car with door unlocked – one per every six these days – saunter towards it, ask for directions, on the passenger side, grab the handle, spring the latch. Jump in. Gun with silencer to the neck – not the head where it could slide along the hair – but the neck where you could lodge it snugly into the flesh. Grab the keys. Reach for the driver-side doorhandle, pop it open, shove the shivering one on to the street. One shot to the head. Jam the car into gear, obey all the traffic rules: no speeding. Just a quick turn down Reynolds, left on Quincy, into Macroy's garage. Quick spray-paint. Plates changed. Out again on to Quincy, three turns, on to the Merritt Parkway northbound, take the second exit, a right off the off-ramp. Three warehouses down. Into the back lot for the drop-off: $500.

That was how you found money in Northport. In a place with no money, Crapshoot did well.

He had talent.

Everyone told him so. Nicknamed Crapshoot because he chalked his talent up to luck, the name had stuck, because the luck had too. He'd only been arrested twice, never even said a rude word – exquisitely polite. He was a genius, others thought. He was willing to concede them that diagnosis. But only on a thousand-dollar day.

Today would be a thousand-dollar day. No problem.

He went into Dunkin' Donuts for a coffee. There was Reg, guarding the papers and a bottle of gin at ten in the morning.

'Reg, wake it up.' His head was down on the Formica table.

Crapshoot moved to the counter and took his coffee, light. This was his only addiction. He never touched drugs, his one beer years ago had made him retch, he had no stomach for most sweet foods. He was healthy and proud of it. He'd been tested for TB twice – negative. Crapshoot's life was ordered. He was successful. He was a clean carjacker and there weren't too many of those. That was what passed for genius in Northport: quick hands that didn't shake with addiction.

He had an investment plan, dumped a thousand a month into a savings account across the Massachusetts border, bought stocks through a discount broker. He was strange, on the street or anywhere else, but he liked it that way. He didn't pay any taxes for his street work, but he did for his legit taxi driving which he did two days a week. Life was pretty for Crapshoot. He never bet on the horses, never spent, never squandered a word or an opportunity. He was clean-cut and well groomed, wore suits he picked up at second-hand stores, always a flower in the lapel, a pink carnation, until it died. Murray's Flowers ordered the carnations specially for him – even in the dead of winter.

This was the way of the street that Crapshoot knew.

He passed the crack addicts every day, knew all their names. They knew his. The cops knew him as the scammer he was, figured him to be a small-time pimp, but didn't know about the cars. No, the cars were private. The way to beat the cops, he learned long ago, was to give them something to pigeonhole you with and then walk in the back door. Like this: he was thought to be a pimp so he talked up the pathetic, stockinged girls on the corner of Wainright & Main at three in the morning. Everyone thought he was their pimp. They didn't have one, but appreciated his attention, because he often gave them twenties for nothing. The cops would drive by.

'How goes it, Billy? Slow night?'

'Yes, Rudy.' He knew all the cops by name.

'Good, Billy. Keep it that way.'

But then he was gone, into that night, a night only slow to those who didn't see.

The carjacking problem in Northport was bad. But there were so many amateurs that the cops felt they were winning. Crapshoot worked with a ring, with pros, and the cars were on their way down to Florida within an hour of the grab. The amateurs got caught while the pros kept on pulling cars off the street. Crapshoot only worked when it was right. Waiting out tough periods when the police worked overtime. He knew every unmarked car, every shift change, every sign that something wasn't right. It would be hard to finger Crapshoot.

He was looking to expand, maybe into legit businesses. Maybe the donut business.

'Where's Marty?'

'He's not in,' said the counterboy.

'Tell him Crapshoot wants a piece of his next franchise. Tell him it's time.'

'What?'

'Just tell Marty, Crapshoot says it's time.'

This was business, Northport style. Car money flowed into drugs two blocks down. Here, car money flowed into mutual funds and then into Dunkin' Donuts franchises. There was a beauty in it, thought Crapshoot, as he walked back on to the sidewalk. America.

It was cold. It would snow tomorrow. He buttoned his overcoat.

There were other ways to make money for sure, but none as sure. He was always looking for new ways. It wasn't greed, he liked to think, but hunger – lust. He thought of it this way: I want what everyone else wants here in Northport, I want everything I can never have. But others, they are content with gin and a little crystal to smoke. I need much more. I need things that people can't imagine.

Crapshoot couldn't even define his needs to himself. But when a Mercedes or Saab came around the corner, looking lost, rich, without a prayer, Crapshoot saw a way to fulfil them. There were other things he did too. Life had so many opportunities. No one saw half of them except him. That's what amazed him about the world. Why when someone saw $80,000 worth of metal crawling slowly down Morone Street did they not think of that as an opportunity? He was not sure. But what mattered was staying in the game, every game, making money, finding new games.

Look at that, he thought, picking up a flier on the sidewalk outside Dunkin' Donuts, *Gold Bought & Sold*. This was the kind of low-class pawn operation he didn't approve of. It wasn't industry. There was nothing creative about it. Buying and selling. Trash.

Across the street, six men stood around a trashcan bonfire. He walked past. He knew all the men, and waved formally, smiling, with dignity and stature – as the President does on a whistle stop. And it was fitting, for though he hadn't been elected democratically, he was the totem of the street's executive branch here in Northport.

Crapshoot headed to his office, the taxi stand on Barrow, where he was friends with the dispatcher. As the only cabby in a suit, Crapshoot garnered a certain amusement and respect in the office. He stepped to the back where the dispatcher let him use a desk in return for a small fee. It was a good, anonymous place. It had everything he needed: some quiet, a watercooler, decent heat, and a trapdoor that led to a back exit even the dispatcher didn't know about. Deeply ingrained in him was the philosophy that you always needed two ways out of any one place.

He opened the local paper. This was the time for morning deals, business, and the like. It wasn't the right time for cars, that he knew. He always had the right instincts about cops. He called it his eighth sense, his sixth being for money, his seventh for power.

'What're thinkin', Billy? Wanna work today?'

Crapshoot looked up at the dispatcher, a man of bulbous bad looks and cigarette stains. He never left his seat by the door. But he was a good dispatcher. He knew where all the cabs were at any given time. *Chess*, he liked to call it. *A good dispatcher needs to know where every cab is at every minute. Get the work out, that's the only way*, he would say.

'Nothing today, thanks. I have deals to do.'

'What's new, Billy? I have deals too. I have to deal with you.' He chuckled. A bad joke to himself was all he needed to get through the day.

Crapshoot stepped outside. It was cold and otherworldly, as if this world weren't cold enough.

A car made its way down Barrow and turned on Acorn. That meant Morone Street was next. But he had planned to change streets tonight. The cops would be watching Morone by now. He walked up a few paces. No cops. He couldn't let it get by Morone. And he knew there were no cops. It was a shift change. He skipped joyously across the street. He called to the garage.

'I've got sticky fingers, baby.'

That was Crapshoot's phrase for a hit. He loved it. Poetic. The poetry of all things – the profit of all things. That was his mantra.

On Morone, the car was slow, uncertain. It was a kelly green Jag. Perfect. Crapshoot checked for unmarkeds and moved to his corner. He adjusted his carnation. It was wilting terribly. He would get a new one in an hour.

Crapshoot liked what he saw. In the Jag was a suburban John looking for a whore. Probably an upstanding citizen from upstanding Westbridge over the border. That made it easier in every way. He could even do without killing the guy. The John would never go to the police: too embarrassing to explain what happened. But Crapshoot knew he *would* kill the John, even though he was probably a father, or about to be one. Crapshoot was careful, after all. Businesses had to be run tip-top. And this was a professional business. Business was business and deals were deals.

Soon, new deals would take hold of him and he wished the moment onward. The need to expand kept gnawing at his heart, right below the carnation. Something new, something tremendous: to own *someone* as well as something. That was the ultimate scam. It was a joke with penny ante fraud – practised all too easily. It was even too simple with killing. That was the cheapest of all. A shot to the head proved nothing about who was boss. But to own a victim, really, he would have to look deeper. Into their soul...

He stepped to the car and popped the latch. It gave easily. *Groovy, groovy,* he thought. Business was good.

3

Why did she not know him?

Once, when she and Paul had been on vacation in Nova Scotia, she paused as she stood putting away her belongings in the bureau in the inn's bedroom. She looked at him organising his own underwear, toiletries, magazines. Amazing how absurdly fastidious he was that he needed to put everything away as soon as he arrived. It had always been the same routine on vacation: arrive, check in, unpack, undress, ejaculate as fast as a snake's tongue inside her, nap. But now, as she watched the steps of his ritual and focused on what was inevitable, she realised how distanced she was from his activity. Each person's rituals are so hopelessly private that the very privacy of them is lonely. She watched him put away his belt. And his cigars. Then the shoddy, old portable radio which he was never without.

Why did she not know him?

There, in the Nova Scotian twilight, by the seashore she had never known and never visited before, was a man she had been married to five years and knew less than the shells on the beach down below.

When he fondled her later that evening, before they went down for drinks by the fire, she shrank away from him with rigid spite. He had barely noticed her reticence, masturbating quietly beside her in a state of half consciousness until he came on the fresh hotel sheets. Then he'd slept until he woke, hungry, an hour later. During that hour she had lain next to him, watching him – the skin as yellow as cigarette stains, the waxy lips thin as threads.

At drinks they'd met a couple from New Zealand. The wife was young and Paul liked looking at her. The husband was wheezy and bloodshot, with an unpleasant way of sitting at an angle so that his ass spilled out from under him. Caitlin had taken to the wife immediately. *How is it*, Caitlin asked giddy from the stout beer she wasn't used to, when they were alone for a minute, *that you manage to love him?*

The wife had nodded, as if expecting the question. She rolled her eyes and tossed her head back with a confidence Caitlin found attractive. She answered something that Caitlin never forgot and tried even to record in her journal the next day, though sober and without memory:

He is for me what fathers are for many girls. Heroic, pathetic, a failure, yet the only one they will ever love. He is rich and he supports me. He buys me anything I want. Then there is his need: he leers at me with a lust unmatched. He appreciates my breasts more than I do. He begs me for everything. Then there is his will, which leaves everything to me. It's legal, binding and videotaped in front of four barristers. It's drafted on elegant parchment. It disowns his own daughter.

There had been other moments of illumination, of inquiry, of philosophy, but what really convinced her of her aloneness in the world was the time she and Paul had decided to buy a hot tub. It was a deluxe model, with redwood and beautiful detailing. It arrived on a truck and was lowered into its resting place in the sunroom. Caitlin looked at it with suspicion. She associated hot tubs with champagne and sex and California and occasional hashish – but not with Paul. What *was* he doing with this? What were they *both* doing with it? She pictured Paul in the tub but she could not picture herself alongside him. She pictured him groping for her leg underwater, but her nowhere to be found. He had misunderstood her in buying the hot tub.

When he came home that night, delighted at the successful installation, he immediately took to filling the tub and watching the steam rise and fog up the sunroom glass. Then he, in a spontaneity unsuited to either his voice or his naked form or his oversized feet, stripped and slid his pale body into the tub and groaned with pleasure. She'd never heard him so ecstatic and the sound of his pleasure made her ill with sorrow. He had never sounded so happy, even within her, while she had never been quite happy at all, with or without him, as long as she could recall. With the water, the steam and the rising vapours, he was at home, and at rest. And there, without his need signalling to her as it once had briefly, she was very much alone. Caitlin stooped to feel the water's silky warmth, watched the pearls of foam collecting on the surface, and felt as if drowning. Half wanting it.

But she stayed alive, something that to Caitlin seemed as much by accident as a blessing, like a fluorescent light that flickers and flickers and flickers without igniting the gases that sit coldly within it.

For Caitlin there was one way out and she saw it passing in the strollers in the ice-cream parlours in Darien, with yellow bootees in some cases and blue in others, sometimes with blankets clutched in a small fist, often with a pacifier oozing with saliva and early dissatisfaction; she noticed it in barbershops atop great white plastic horses that serve as chairs, with multi-coloured lollies in their mouths as rewards for that first shearing; once, she noticed it, all forlorn and none too Fairfield County, dirty and undernourished with a scraped knee and the trappings of squalor – but that was in the ghettos of Northport, where Caitlin got stuck when she took a wrong turn off the Merritt Parkway. And even that, that *too* appeared a way out; in summer it presented itself around poolsides: laughing, running, tumbling, flipping in with a splash, diving deep, and then coming up for air with all the urgency of small, spent lungs. A child was the only way out.

She imagined the lullabies she would sing if given the chance: crooning, utterly indulgent, melancholy. After all, she would not raise an independent child, but one absolutely devoted to her, one as desperate for her love as she would be for its presence. The idea made her dizzy with excitement when it occurred to her in that way, in Technicolor, with all the pastel blues and pinks of babydom pasted on the backdrop, causing her to spin and spin and wearily collapse, and hug her belly, hoping for it to swell along with her excitement.

4

Page twelve.

There was a small ad soliciting sperm donors at $50 a sample – *Inseminology Institute*. That could be easy money, thought Crapshoot, tearing the ad out neatly. He was going to put it in his file for safe keeping but then thought better of it and left it on the desk. He'd never donated sperm. The idea didn't immediately appeal to him, but something gnawed at him – in the same spot – just below the stiff carnation where he imagined his heart to be.

He turned again to the newspaper.

The paper was the starting point for most business deals. A business deal worked like this: down the page there was a much bigger advertisement for a medium-sized furniture outlet in Hartford. Crapshoot scanned the ad copy: typical, banal. The spread was big, a full page, an expensive ad. He called up the outlet and asked their address and what their selection was like for convertible sofas with a stain-free, plush upholstery. Then he requested to speak to the manager and asked more questions about the styles, selection, prices, colours, accessories. Finally, he inquired about a layaway plan, the possibility of acquiring a store credit card, penalties for late payment, discounts on large orders, and the radius of free delivery. He politely thanked the manager. It was the right-sized business – big enough to have several employees and too much paperwork, small enough to have lax controls and an unprofitable dose of disorganisation.

Crapshoot called the local paper's display advertising department, introducing himself as a small businessman wondering whether he could afford a full-page ad to promote his burgeoning chain of auto lube shops. Prices started at $1200 for a one-colour, one-day run, replied the saleswoman.

Could he pay for the ad in a week or so once his cash flow improved?

No problem. The paper customarily required only a 10 per cent deposit up front. He would be billed for the balance later.

Crapshoot hung up and started drafting the invoice. He had a stock invoice pad that he kept locked in the desk drawer allotted for his use. He fed one of the triplicate forms through the old electric typewriter and punched out the following:

One full page, one colour, one day display.	$1200
Deposit, credited Jan. 16. Thank you.	$120
Balance due.	$1080

He typed the address of the furniture outlet in the square on the invoice reserved for that purpose and folded the bill so that the address would show through the cellophane window of the business envelope.

He also enclosed a professional return envelope, self-addressed with one of his many post office box addresses and postage metered for a normal business-sized envelope.

Six weeks later he would check the post office box, a

temporary one in Stamford, and find a $1200 cheque made out to Eagle Media Group, the dummy business concern of which he was sole owner under an alias. He would then cash the cheque at his bank branch in Stamford, along with the six or seven other cheques he would receive from similar projects, then close the account and the post office box in one day, and start up again somewhere else. The furniture outlet would only discover the error several months later, after the real bill arrived and an audit was performed.

Crapshoot would move into a different line of business soon. This one was becoming less profitable as time wore on and accounts payable began to tighten up. It was always important to get out of the right line of business at the right time.

Everything was a racket, thought Crapshoot, once you knew the angle. He could deal in anything given half a chance. Selling was selling. He prided himself on being able to sell things that weren't there. To sell a liability, a debt, to a furniture outlet where none existed: that was not flim-flam, it was art. The glory in selling things that didn't exist was that what you were really selling was an idea, and that, to Crapshoot, was beautiful. Cars were fine, and he liked the thrill of it. Quick money. High risk. Excitement that made his gut quiver. There was nothing like pulling off a car job, because you turned that car into its alter ego so quickly that it made your head spin. And then it was on its way to Florida for early retirement. It went like clockwork. And clocks need to be wound up to work.

Money. Crapshoot was in love with it. Crisp bills, or worn. Shiny gold, or dull. High stocks, or low. Money to him was not appliances, or fancy yachts sailing on the Caribbean. Money was inspiration. A goal. A fetish.

Selling was about money and money was about being.

Without money, lots of it, he couldn't be. Since the equation was that simple, so was the calculation. Crapshoot would make money and money would make him.

Human innovation. The poetry of that phrase had stuck on Crapshoot. He liked to think on it. When man first sent a satellite out of the solar system, Crapshoot had thought: *That's beautiful, but the real beauty in it is thinking how plain it will be in a hundred years.* Crapshoot liked to dream of new ventures and new adventures. To him, the two were linked. Money and pioneers. Experimentation and profit. He had wanted, years ago, to provide seed capital for a biotechnology firm. With a few hired brains and his bankroll, they could've defined the next frontier. As it was, he stuck to humble Northport and waited.

5

'Your sperm are like medusae. They are snake-headed, ugly, deformed, oddly insolent, lazy, treacherous – sickly. They are, frankly, biologically unfit.'

Caitlin looked at Paul. It would be hard to take, this kind of talk. But that's what they were here for. To drink in reality. Caitlin looked at her husband, so dapper in his woollen suit, so controlled in his manner – so outwardly immune to this reproach of his spermatozoa. She didn't want to hear it any more than he did. To hear that your husband, the man you picked, is as good at impregnating as he is at lactating, isn't pleasant. Primevally, it's painful. For evolution tells you to pick the strongest of males, the one with not only sperm, but sacred sperm. To know that you have failed in your evolutionary mission is to know that you have failed to carry out the master plan, to propagate the species. It's failure, plain and simple.

The doctor was gesticulating from his chair, dramatically illustrating the deformed condition of Paul's sperm with violent thrusts of the forefinger. He was, after all, a fertility guru. As such, he could command the attention of those without child. Caitlin looked at the brass plate on the desk: Richard Dotterweich, MD, PhD – the series of letters after the name almost fertile themselves in their impressiveness.

'Sperm are elegant, lithe beings in their normal state. They meander, swim, pulsate with life's strength. They are single-minded in their purpose. They descend upon the female egg with irrepressible delight. A healthy sperm is God's goodness – a tail, a head, a healthy dose of genetic gel – the beginning of all beginnings. A healthy sperm is fantasy, miracle. Sperm in motion are the most elegant of human phenomena: rhapsodic, graceful – a ballet.

'Yet, sperm with coiled tails, multiple heads, stubborn indifference, malformed physiques, unaccustomed sloth, ineffective motility, these sperm are useless.' Dotterweich pulled from his desk drawer two vials, cloudy with viscous ejaculate, and held them to the light. 'You and I cannot tell the difference between these samples. But, while one is the meaning of life incarnate, one has no meaning at all.'

Paul stuttered slightly, then spoke. 'Dr Dotterweich, I feel driven to apologise to you, to our unborn child, to Caitlin. To *somebody*.'

Dotterweich waved the air. 'One cannot apologise for biological conditions. That is like apologising for your eye colour. But don't mistake me. It *is* frailty of which we speak. Nature has no forgiveness for frailty. Frailty is separated out, like chaff.' His East European accent put a special emphasis on *frailty*. Some symbolic, invisible umlaut had descended on the word. 'Nature has no mercy. How could it? Nature is not *about* mercy. Nature is about natural selection – about selecting the best and the brightest from the masses, about plucking beauty from the coterie of ugliness that clings to this world. Yet, with technology we often trick nature. We preserve poor gene pools into the next generation.

MISBEGOTTEN

'Take, for example, insulin treatment for diabetics. Without regular insulin injections, serious diabetics would die an early death before bearing children. With insulin we keep the diabetic alive, long enough to spawn the next generation. This preserves the gene for diabetes in the gene pool. We are preserving bad genes. Call it, perhaps, de-evolution.

'It is possible, of course, to fool nature for the better. To use nature's own tools against her. Yes, indeed. It is far from an improbability. It is the present. That's what we do here at our institute. We only select the most excellent sperm. Perfectly formed. Superbly motile. Ideally suited to tackle the human egg, to convey exquisite chromosomal information, to craft the next generation. Indeed, it is the institute's pride that our chromosomal material is prime stock: programmed for intelligence, health, even beauty.'

For Caitlin, Dotterweich's lecture was evangelism. His energy was motivating, his procreative fervour compelling.

In church as a young girl she'd listened to the minister's words on the first anniversary of her mother's and her bird's death. That day, Caitlin had left the house to pick flowers and had happened upon a thatch of moss straddling a tree base. There, simply, lay a dead bird. It amused her at first to think of a bird sleeping so soundly in such a comfortable spot. But the stillness of it disturbed her and she wasn't quite sure whether birds did sleep at all anyway. Death didn't occur to her. She'd never before happened upon death. Except in fairy-tale vocabulary the word didn't appear real. Maybe it wasn't real. Yet, when she poked the bird with the toe of her small white sneaker, the body yielded and then fell back. How odd to be a body and not act as a body would – to not have any motion of itself, only outside itself. Her father, who hunted for a hobby, had held her hand as he explained that the bird would not wake. Then he dug a small grave and allowed Caitlin to fill it and cross two fern fronds on top. She said a prayer at her daddy's direction and returned to the house to play. Only when a small coldness gripped her later in the evening did she ask her father when she could see the bird again. When he replied *never*, that the bird had left this world and moved on, Caitlin asked if Mommy and Daddy would ever do such a thing. *Mommy and Daddy love you, darling. They're not going anywhere.* Caitlin had run off to play. An hour later her mother was killed in a head-on collision with a drunk driver. Caitlin knew her mother had decided to leave because she didn't love her darling any more. That much was clear. A year later in church on the anniversary of both deaths, the minister had confirmed that idea:

> *The real essence of man is not of this world, but of a heavenly place of good works and redemption. A mere shadow resides with us on earth, tending to God's ministrations here. When the true usefulness of man is called upon, it must meet its calling above. Only above.*

This was, to Caitlin, a disappointment. To have lived with a mere shadow of her mother was bizarre, horrible.

Her father remained well acquainted with death. He continued to hunt for many years. His guns were very important to him. He used to lecture Caitlin on the proper use of guns and, when she was older, taught her how to shoot. She remembered her father saying, as he once loaded the gun and explained to her how a safety catch worked, 'You never take this down until you're ready to fire. Taking off the safety is like having a child. Once you do it, you'd better know what you're doing.' Then he pointed the gun at the target and fired. The blast shocked her. She recoiled along with the gun. 'And be careful of guns around people. But if you must shoot a man, look him in the eyes when you pull the trigger: you can't shoot a man who has any goodness in his heart when you look him in the eyes.'

Flesh and blood held very little over death. Yet flesh and blood were the topic at hand. Cellular flesh; genetically combined blood. A few drops of potent semen dabbed to the base of a luminescent egg: life, artificially realised. Surely, in the flesh and blood that would grow test-tubed and manufactured there would be something more resilient than that which emerged through nature's unadorned grace. This much she could hope for. This much Dotterweich could – *would* – engineer.

'Eugenics perhaps. Why not?' Dotterweich stood. His desk chair buckled with relief. 'The alternative is mass degradation, pitiful progeny, Piltdown man. That is why we labour to collect the best and preserve the best. And deliver the best. To you. You would want a child stronger, better, I assume, than each of you. A child of prime stock, equipped for life's reversals, the tedious and the treacherous both. Your child will be excellent. Would you want it any other way?'

Paul looked up humbly. 'We want a child.'

'Of course a child. But not *a* child, *the* child. Had you been endowed with viable sperm, Mr Bourke, you would have sloppily slapped together a child of the type that inhabits this planet routinely: anachronistic, devolved, pathetic in its frailty, flawed, bitterly flawed. But here. Well, well.' Dotterweich tapped the desk. 'Here, we find the perfect genetic complement to your wife's DNA. We, in effect, do what nature does imperfectly: link the perfect strands in happy communion. It is delightful to contemplate it.'

Caitlin looked at Dotterweich. The mad scientist would engineer their baby, their very own Frankenstein. How romantic. How desperate. How *delightful*.

There was a stain on Dotterweich's lab coat, just below the middle button, just above the uncertain waistline. It was a small grey-yellow stain and Caitlin wondered whether it was semen – his or someone else's – or just mustard from lunch. Here, all fluids seemed equally potent and impotent, equally capable of being important to life or not.

Caitlin recalled the first time she tasted semen. Eighteen and eager to learn she positioned herself between the prom date's legs and just decided to start licking. She was prepared, when she finally enveloped his penis in her mouth. There was the humiliation of his telling her to go easy with her teeth. But for the salty taste, the humid clime between loins, the frenzied bucking with pleasure that accompanied the ejaculation, and utter lack of enjoyment on her part, she was not prepared. Relief had been the dominant emotion, when she assessed the fact that she couldn't have been impregnated via the oesophagus. So, first sex was a sex of pleasure in sterility. And if pleasure could come no other way, then pleasure in the perpetual relief of not procreating would suit her fine. Now, procreation was the goal and pleasure stood aside. Who could have predicted such an abnormal sex life for such a normal girl, she thought? Or was it the essence of normal, the sad underpinning of a sterile society, as Paul liked to maintain?

In the study at night she would often cry. But for what, she didn't know. She had read that unexplained bouts of crying are indicative of clinical depression. Yet, the wonder of tears without purpose inspired her. It was as though her life was so chronically important that something would eventually *have* to give – some satellite in this cosmology of unhappiness would implode and gift its dusty salvation to her planet down below.

And then there was Paul.

With his bloodshot eyes and humiliation and wretched excuses and sad, sad demeanour in doctors' offices, Paul was very much her husband. But since she knew him little and wished him to be better, Caitlin yearned for something else.

'Like so, we will begin. I will transmit to you a list of anonymous donor profiles. Each and every detail. Banalities such as height and weight, shoe size. Totalities like religious background, socioeconomic status, education, health, the like. And you will pick. Beware! You are picking your child. We will double-check matches that we compute will combine nicely with the various permutations of genetic material in Mrs Bourke's egg. So you need not worry about that. Of course, it is a highly technical process. One which you could not accomplish on your own in any case.

'Once you have the profiles, perhaps thirty or forty in all, you will inform us of your choice, and the clinicians will arrange for the insemination, which is indeed a simple process. You will have to sign various legal forms and then we will watch the fantastical process of a child being launched. We will, of course, monitor your gestation completely. We will perform traditional tests like amniocentesis and ultrasounds. Finally, we will do our own selective tests to determine more precisely the health of the child. If there is any problem, it will be determined within the first trimester. If so, the decision as to an abortion will of course be yours alone. In six years of this process, we have had wonderful success, largely because our gene pool is so carefully screened to begin with. We go to great effort and expense to recruit superb semen.

'Any questions?'

Caitlin slung one leg over the other and touched her finger to her cheek. 'Dr Dotterweich, does a client ever get to meet the donor?'

Paul looked sleepy, wistfully exhausted. He crossed his legs in conjunction with his wife. Dotterweich stared out the window on to the suburban hillside. The entry sign was partially obscured but the letters were still readable, INSEMINOLOGY INSTITUTE in bold black type. A grey blanket of old snow looked menacing and provoked uncomfortable thoughts of the journey home. The night threatened its early descent and the trees swayed with a gust that came along with a mild whisper.

'Mrs Bourke, if I were to pluck your eggs one at a time and distribute hundreds of them to the populace for controlled breeding, would you want those recipients, all of them, meeting you?'

Caitlin thought about it. She gazed out the window too. There was nothing there to speak of. Only a Connecticut winter's moodiness and Dotterweich's profile, so sure of itself. 'I don't know.'

'Well, we do, Mrs Bourke. You wouldn't. And they *don't*. Life must emerge on its own, without traditional, oozingly sentimental concerns for biological constancy. You will never know the donor. And that will be best. For Paul will be the father. No one else. And you will be a family. There will be no one else to threaten that happy dynamic.'

In the gusts of wind, there was again a mild whisper. Caitlin listened carefully, but it didn't speak to her.

6

Half-dead, bleeding, the man begged to be spared.

Crapshoot considered it. Another shot would be risky and time was slipping, along with the filthy runoff, through the gutters on Morone. A minute and a half to make it to the garage at the most. A pop to the head would be messy at this range. But no, the street. It wouldn't be empty for long. And he'd been seen. Crapshoot squeezed the trigger. Such convulsive reflex, such ugly bloodiness, such condescension towards life. He gave it only a moment's thought. No more.

It was a Volvo – but the nicest model. Leather interior, a tape deck, good acceleration. At Macroy's, Crapshoot opened the glove compartment while the boys painted and did the plates. A toy doll fell out. An unattractive troll-like thing with orange hair. So it had been a father back there, begging for mercy on the tarmac, arms extended in a bloody call of uncle.

Well, the little ones would have to raise themselves. That was the rule of the jungle. Crapshoot subscribed to it. How ridiculous anyway, all the coddling that undermined a child's true strength: private schools, parental indulgence, presents on every major holiday except VJ Day; miniature pump Nikes at ten, tennis camp in Florida at eleven, on the shrink's couch at twelve. This was the progression. It was softening – demeaning. Crapshoot scorned it. The very idea of a family life in this culture. It sickened him.

He was tempted to have a child just to lead it, just to teach it the real ways of the world, just to gain control of it – of something. But he would need a mother for that. Why not? A mother to control as well ... a mother to control through her child. He remembered the semen donor ad that lay crinkled in his wallet.

The gnawing feeling came again, but he laughed and ran the last light before the Merritt Parkway by mistake. A police cruiser tagged him and flashed its dome lights in the rearview.

Crapshoot whistled. *Lovely, lovely.* For Crapshoot, this was the decision: chance it that the carjacking hadn't been reported yet and pull over. Or, outrun him. The plates were changed and he had the new registration, but the cop would know him. *What a honeysuckle mess*, he said to himself, recalling the line his grandmother would've attached to it. He pulled over just to the right of the viaduct, adjusted his collar and propped up the carnation in his pocket. *If you can't be good, look good.*

It was tidy enough. One cop, alone, in the cruiser. Crapshoot waited for him to look down and start logging the plate number into the computer. He counted to three. Then he jammed it into reverse. The impact hit hard. He jumped out of the passenger door and ran down the viaduct path, all the way to the edge of the old reservoir. There he knew the trees and the edges of the shanty town that gave way to bonfires after dark. It was cold. His lungs ached with the effort. But he was free.

And the night was a grand time. You could only really be free at night. Free from the sunlight, free from the bustle and clatter of the day. Free from the surveillance of the police. He settled into a small grove of bushes that would provide ample cover. On the ground were a few used condoms and shards of glass, beer cans and hypodermics.

Crapshoot watched for the cop. Nothing. He was probably still adjusting his neck from the collision.

Crapshoot skipped along down the reservoir edge until he came to the vast steps that descended to Cannon Park. Once there, he waved to the drug dealers and made it back to Morone Street in time to see the ambulance and police cruisers assembled to take the dead father away.

To botch a job that badly. Maybe he was losing his touch. He looked down at his hands. They weren't shaking but his legs were tired and his head dizzy. Maybe he *was* losing his touch. Or his timing.

He walked up to the small crowd that had formed around the ambulance. Officer Tenley was there. Crapshoot saluted him playfully.

'Watch it, Billy. I'm not in the mood. We got another carjack here.'

'I can tell. I see the blood and the tyre marks.'

'Jesus, Billy, you'd make a good detective, know that? Now get lost somewhere.'

'Tell me one thing.'

'What's that?'

'Who was it?'

'I don't know. Middle-aged guy.'

'A father?'

'Probably. Why?'

'Oh, it's a sad sight, that's all. Kids need their parents, wouldn't you say?'

Officer Tenley didn't answer him. The call came over

for the car recovered on Bigelow. The driver was at large, in the woods, no description available.

Yes, kids need their parents. It was a sad scene. But all the better to breed strong beings. No indulgences in Northport. No time for that. It was the bravest of new worlds. Crapshoot walked over to the Dunkin' Donuts.

If it was going to be a thousand-dollar day, he'd better get going.

MISBEGOTTEN

In the oblong of her bedroom, she decided to masturbate.

The bed was unmade. The sheets cool, unsettled. She started with a song. It was something she hummed to herself, an erotic inspiration. The undressing had to be ceremonious and the lights dim. It was daylight but she'd lowered the shades.

She'd once used a mirror but had been too embarrassed to watch herself. Besides, her imagination, a projection of unmatched fascination, provided her with all measure of abandon. There was no need for ocular stimulus. She rubbed the cotton of her T-shirt against her nipples to harden them. Her breasts were small, compact, conservatively positioned, B-cups. As a teen she had tried to grow them with ardent thoughts of germination. Hopelessly, she'd watched them remain as they were. Now she was proud of their sprightly loyalty.

Caitlin had a catalogue of fantasies. She waited for one to descend upon her. This was all part of the ceremony, the elaborate steps without which there would be no orgasm. It appeared: the startling abstract of a man with no face. He laid his hand upon her breast where moments earlier she had touched herself. The shock of his touch made her eyes roll backwards. He caressed her, undressed her. Again and again. Then, savage with his purpose, he was behind her and entering her. She went numb.

In her fantasy she changed the design.

Now she was the Amazonian Princess, formally disguised as befitted her mission, in spare jungle garb. Her costume, now ripped asunder and laid beside her, evidenced the ravaging that conducted itself in a slow, monotonous greed.

Above, on the superficial, she was being raped and used. But within her understanding, in that place where her fantasies and knowledge resided, she was the Amazonian Princess. Her mission, as it had been explained to her on that moonless night that had come before all other moonless nights, directed her to salvage the sperm, the most vibrant genetic material, from the strongest of all the male chieftains. She would carry that chromosomal imprint back to the tribe of Amazon and be welcomed as a hero. This was her mission. The numbness disappeared. The moment of moments was upon her. She gasped with pleasure.

In the dark room, her heartbeat accompanied her. The digital clock read 4:24. Paul would be home soon. She set about straightening up the bed. A neat bed was important to Paul.

8

On this, the shortest day of the year, Billy Crapshoot felt the cold, even in his cab, even while masturbating. When sunrise and sunset come so close together that they can be knitted with a cross-stitch, things look bleak. Money was tight. No good cars. Too many cop patrols. Morone Street was being watched. McKellan too. So what else was there to do?

Crapshoot had reached for the tissues on the dash, taken the bondage magazine out of the glove compartment, turned to his recent favourite photo and jacked off. A buxom blonde was whipping a small, scholarly man who was naked except for boxers and a bowtie. Crapshoot ejaculated within a minute and the cum hit the dash.

It occurred to him that somewhere around here he could get paid for this sad little ritual. At $50 a pop, he'd be glad to do the work. But he'd thought and thought on it and the $50 seemed the least of it. To give a little of his next generation to the common good. And then ... well ... to make that good less common and more his own. A vague plan started to form.

He shifted into park and went for a ride.

At the light Sedge was at his window. Sedge was an addict. Crapshoot gave him a dollar. What a different economy these people had off the crack and on it. Without it, a dollar could go a day. But for someone under the influence, dollars were only as meaningful as their presence. That was the trick of addiction: it made dollars have no soul to themselves – no history, no staying power. The time value of money had no meaning in Northport, where the only purpose of any sort of investment was to make the next hour disappear.

Crapshoot decided to run up to Stamford to get a fare at the train station. When it was slow and there was no money, sometimes the only thing to do was run up to Stamford and take a fare from the station to one of the big suburban homes. He liked the ride for the novelty and sightseeing.

Big suburban homes and dreams were good for the soul, mused Crapshoot. He was the first to admit his love for this part of Americana. He liked to ride slowly past the classically quiet streets, the stately trees, the well-zoned parcels. It was best in summer when the bare bones of prosperity were plainly visible. He would admire this bit of shrubbery, that screened-in patio. He respected the quiet, sturdy wealth. Confident in his very own abilities to mint his very own gold, Crapshoot was not resentful of others' success. He welcomed it as all part and parcel of his own bubbling economy. Each car in every drive was a potential piece of his own future holdings. Currency littered the streets. Who could resent that which was by all rights his own? As he drove, he cared not at all for the human dramas that played themselves out here regularly. What he craved were glimpses of material. Not just cars: boats on trailers, poised for the abbreviated odyssey down to the coast on the other side of the throughway; barbecue grills bright and shiny, ready for the ritual of the Fourth; elegantly appointed poolsides, with all the trappings;

picture windows, providing views of the wallpaper, the credenzas; welcome mats, so welcoming in their kemptness; sparkling tricycles, for a new generation of riches; occasional tennis courts, impressive in their lack of use, luxuriously waiting.

Yes, Crapshoot liked this world. Very much.

It wasn't uncommon for him to value properties as he drove by, like an overzealous tax assessor, possessed of his mission. Or, a rogue real estate agent on fraudulent turf, he computed his fanciful commissions. Sometimes like a prospective buyer, he knocked on doors, asked questions, toured the grounds, pledged a down-payment, then drove away. Any role that permitted access, propriety, a comfortable sense of home, pleased Crapshoot.

He eased the cab down into the lot of the train station. A man in an overcoat with a small brown satchel flagged him down. He was stooped against the wind and the flurries.

'Where to?' Crapshoot looked the fare over in the rearview and propped up his carnation so that it could be seen. The fare was older, with glasses, fogged over in the cold.

'116 South Kenney.'

'It's not a beach day, for sure.'

The fare removed his glasses and rubbed his hands. 'No. No, it's not.'

'But I get fresh flowers, any season. You see?'

The fare nodded.

'*I* am always in season.'

'That's a good way to look at things. I have always tried to feel that way. I'm afraid my climate is more deciduous – I tend to fall off when it's time to fall off and then grow back when nature gives me an ample watering. But indeed, these days the ample waterings seem to come later and later in the season. The doctor says it's all due to a weak heart, but I know it's due to a weak soul – one dissipated by lack of discipline.'

They were making the turn on to South Kenney. Crapshoot slowed down and looked in the rearview. *Well, probably the breast pocket. Tough one. Oh well. But a nice guy. No need to break heads. Gently, gently.*

'What do you do for a living?' asked Crapshoot.

'I'm a poet. A decent one. And you?'

'Well, two guesses for you. You could get rich.' Crapshoot looked the poet in the eye in the mirror. 'You a gambling man?'

The poet smiled. 'For sure. To me, winning's fine, losing's OK. Not being in the hand – well, that's the only dull thing. I think you could say that makes me a gambling man.'

'Well then. Put your money where your mouth is.'

Crapshoot snuck a glance to the rearview. The poet patted his hip pocket gently – instinctively. 'I keep my money closer to its inspiration. So, good sir, what *is* your mission in life?'

Lovely, lovely. Hip pocket. We can do this the easy way.

'Take a guess. Put those poet's wits together, friend, how 'bout it?'

'Well, a detective's instinct would say you're a cabby. A poet's preposterousness, on the other hand, could pin you with anything.'

'You're clever, Mr Poet. I grant you that. Where do you get ideas for your poems, anyway?'

'They say writers should write from experience. I think ideas just roll along – like you and your cab, for example. But experience is definitely the catalyst – like raising my hand to flag you down. I mean if I didn't flag you down, you wouldn't stop and pick me up, now would you? One can't happen without the other.'

'You'd be surprised what happens out here.'

'I'm sure I wouldn't be. I've seen it all. Or at least most of it. Cornelius is the name, Conan J. Cornelius. And you, Mr Cabby?'

'Billy.' The flurries stopped. Crapshoot turned off the wipers. 'You a Stamford man?'

'Oh no. I'm really a city mouse. But I'm staying up here for a few days. I do that in the winter. You know, a snowy Connecticut weekend. What could be better for the soul? My only problem is I don't drive. That always made country living a hardship.'

'You got kids?'

'No. I have my poems. Believe me, they are children: misguided, immature, rebellious, brazen, exceedingly sharp, irreverent – and my greatest passion.'

'You look like a Libra.'

'Is that so?'

'Sure. All fair and formal.'

'Is that so?'

'Let me ask you a question. Does it take a special man to write poetry? Or is it just a roll of the dice?' asked Crapshoot, pulling the cab up at 116 South Kenney, a yellow colonial, small and unpretentious by Stamford standards.

'It is as I've always said: a poet is any man. Just hand him a pen. But don't forget to take away his chance for a normal life.'

'Why thank you, Mr Cornelius.'

He watched the poet put his wallet back in his hip pocket. *Very nice.* Then he left the car in drive and jumped out to open the passenger door. Cornelius looked curiously at Crapshoot's carnation and immaculate suit and then reached inside to grab the satchel.

I am always in season. Crapshoot silently heaved the car

and watched the door hit the fare gently in the hip. He'd done it many times before – a quick helpful hand to the fare's waist. 'Christ, I'm sorry. Didn't put it in park.'

'That's all right. I'm OK.' The fare steadied himself on the icy path. Crapshoot reached out to help him. 'I have weathered many a winter. I'm a tough one. Irish stock.'

'Be good,' admonished Crapshoot with steamy breath. 'It's the shortest day of the year.'

'So much always happens in the shortest day of the year. So little happens in the longest. Don't you think?'

In the cab ride back Crapshoot looked out at the passing homes. It was so calm here, especially on a wintry day. He slowed for a child crossing the road with a sled in tow. The sled was bright red, modern, aerodynamically fit. Sledding was dangerous, thought Crapshoot. That child should have a helmet. Crapshoot turned on the radio to the oldies station and tapped his fingers to the music.

At the red light, he removed a worn wallet from his jacket pocket and ran his finger inside the central fold. One fiver. Nothing. Another five. A driver's licence. Scraps of paper. *A poet, I'll be. Shoulda, shoulda known. Ten bucks to his name. Sadder than sad.* Crapshoot read the name aloud off the driver's licence: Conan J. Cornelius, 145 Bleecker Street #6, New York, NY. He tossed the wallet and kept the licence and the bills. *I'll be. Starving poet. Ten bucks to his name. Not even a bank card. Sadder than sad. Motherfucker's wrong: on the shortest day of the year, nothing happens. That's what you get for trying to be nice.*

Shoulda popped him.

9

'Sex is expensive. In the realm of all species, there is a cost to it. In the differentiation of two sets of genitalia, there is a price – to energy, to complexity, to protein.' Dotterweich expanded his hands broadly to emphasise nature's spendthrift ways. 'Asexual species do much better overall. We are interested in making man asexual, and woman as well. Sexless. With a mere tube we will inseminate you. How much more efficient! The male can go about other biological duties, prepare for nurture and provision, while the female can concentrate on gestation. Had God been more of a visionary, he too would have ordained this.'

Caitlin was more comfortable here without Paul. Yet the biological evangelism of Dotterweich was tiring. Her one goal was to get pregnant. But the profiles Dotterweich had provided were less than inspiring. She had no use for his stable of Yale PhDs or healthy professionals. One profile had initially intrigued her: a neurosurgeon who played classical piano had donated his sperm out of a desire to pass on pure genetic perfection. The arrogance of the ambition had at once impressed and repulsed her. A brilliant doctor, a virtuoso musician – and her son or daughter the offspring of that. That arrogance in a child, though: it could be bad at birthday parties.

The idea of picking a child intrigued her. Caitlin had picked a husband without regard to childrearing and now she was paying for this evolutionary mistake. But to pick now, when the very choice would be void of romance – purely biological – was terrifying.

Dotterweich looked at Caitlin and knew what she was thinking. He had seen it before. As a young woman there are so many possible reasons for that ultimate spousal choice: a walk on the beach, friends, a shared career, an ardently unshared one; or maybe a dent-free dowry, a conspiratorial wink, a flower pink; or better, poems by midnight, kisses by dawn, a love for Chopin, a hatred for Thanksgiving; and then, wonderful love, terrible self-loathing, great sex, or good cooking. The reasons to marry were as numerous as those not to. In the end we marry for some other reason, not the one we think of. Like overeager spectators of a magician's trick, our thoughts follow the red herring, the misdirection, the decoy, the diversion. Our feelings, meanwhile, find their own way, thought Dotterweich sadly.

In the dim light of the office Caitlin pored over the profiles that Dotterweich had given her. Each one included physical characteristics, age, a brief medical history, religious upbringing, race, educational attainment, profession, and reasons for donating sperm. Conspicuously absent in each were those indicators that would give you more than a type: name, address, likes, dislikes, passions even. Without those, Caitlin felt so distanced from these future fathers. Anonymity in sex had never bothered her much. But anonymity in fathering: grave doubts about it began to gnaw at her. The very anonymity of it was what made it possible, she realised. But the notion of knowing a father only by medical speciality was a bit like knowing yourself only by the measurement of your inseam.

So it could be an Episcopalian Johns Hopkins neurosurgeon, with a penchant for golf, or just as easily, an Italian mid-level manager for IBM with an MBA and a decidedly atheist bent. Either way the baby girl or boy that would spring from her womb would love her and cherish her. That was the point. When she thought of *father* though, she thought of more. Perhaps, someone professionless. Someone who just *was*. Someone who didn't step into a uniform and head off to work like everyone else. Somehow, when the professions and the colleges and the medical schools and the degrees were listed there on paper, Caitlin lost interest. Then that person became an ad exec or lawyer or contractor and all of a sudden less interesting.

Caitlin imagined what the first date would be like with each man, after reading his profile. There was the Jewish accountant with a history of chronic colitis and a Master's in Education who earnestly described his desire to help someone have a child. She imagined the slightly wilted tulips he would bring her, his nervous demeanour and twitch, his humble choices from the menu that studiously avoided spicy foods.

The Russian immigrant with a PhD in Physics and occasional gout would court her with a smouldering intelligence and an arrogant distaste for her American naivety.

Then the actor, a younger man with no known medical complications and a BA from Bennington, would take her out for ribs and beer and bring her back to his small studio apartment.

The humanities professor with an overload of degrees, an allergy to penicillin and a mitral valve prolapse would call her twice before getting the courage to ask her out. Finally, with a drink in him and nothing more to lose, he would suggest a trip to New York for an off-Broadway show and a whiskey at the Gramercy Park Hotel. Perhaps he was married. But no matter. They could get a room.

All these men were potential fathers, their silky, liquid potentiality residing in vials at the Inseminology Institute.

She'd considered adoption. That way she could examine it all in advance: examine those tiny toes, the medical charts, and walk away with a baby. But that way you either got a crack-addicted infant or paid for the privilege not to. And then there would be none of Caitlin Bourke there – none of her unique genetic imprint.

Dotterweich spoke: 'Some women feel it is not a choice which they are qualified to make. That it is a godly choice. But you are as qualified as God to make it. God, in all his wisdom, didn't see fit to give you and Paul the option of natural childbirth. Thus, it must be you now who claim the mantle of the responsibility. You will choose your father here, and choose a new beginning. In this you will find redemption, an opportunity to be part of biological invention. You will make the choice.

'Love is universal. So are children. So is mothering, fathering. What are not universal are the permutations of these very things. As many ways there are to give birth as there are sexual positions. In essence the imaginative soul has limitless possibilities. You will draw on that infinite expanse. And I will help you. Paul cannot be as much a part of this process as he would like. He has failed to provide you with an offspring. He feels ashamed. We both understand that shame. It is ugly and deep. Yet science, enlightenment, ingenuity. They step in when humanity fails. We're a part of that.'

Caitlin listened. They were a part of that – part of the

great biological mystery that could garner life from a spoonful of pearly white liquid. Yet the mystery was scary, the conclusion fraught with suspense. A man, then a boy, or a girl. *Think of what can happen,* a voice said to her as she stepped out of Dotterweich's office and slid behind the wheel of the Range Rover. *Think of what can happen.*

MISBEGOTTEN

10

White walls with nothing on them can make anyone nervous. Take a morgue or an insane asylum; take a hospital or a prison.

Or a sperm bank.

Billy Crapshoot adjusted his tie and carnation and walked down the white hallway. A small black sign pointed left to Registration. He followed it. He tried to calm himself. *Love it, love it. They make babies in here.* At the desk was a small man with a goatee and a bowtie.

'Donation?'

Crapshoot nodded.

'Please have a seat over there.' The small man indicated left.

Crapshoot took a seat on the plush leather sofa in the reception area. There were photos on the walls, each an eight-by-ten colour glossy of a recreating family. Some families were on vacation, some were at home. Each was nuclear: a husband, a wife, a boy, a girl, sometimes two. Everyone smiled and radiated health. Even in the content faces and blissful scenes, Crapshoot could find no healthy inspiration of his own for a family.

But his excitement grew at the thought of fathering a child. Anonymously. What really excited him was the thought of the poor mother, left to her own sorry guesswork and sadder fictions as to who he was. While he reeled her in, slowly, slowly – with his own stories, his own borrowed identity. They would love him on the street for this if they could only understand it! It was the ultimate scam. He sat and waited. Touching his carnation, he tried to still his heartbeat.

The small man rose and stepped towards him. 'A donation counsellor will be with you shortly. Can I get you anything while you're waiting?'

'A cup of water would go down nicely.'

The small man pointed blandly to a watercooler. Crapshoot helped himself.

A few minutes later a young lady stepped out of a small doorway down the hallway and called to him, 'Right this way, please.'

In her office there were more familial glossies. In every smile was some sort of lie, mused Crapshoot. Perhaps a lie about incest, or drug addiction, or disease. He looked from the photos to the woman and again to the photos. She looked too young to have her own family. Her auburn hair was cut very short, in a bob. She smiled occasionally, a sweet small smile, which crinkled the corners of her eyes.

'I'm Beth Sorensen. Please make yourself comfortable.'

'Do you have your own family?' He sat.

'No, actually I don't. Some day.' She smiled. 'Let me review with you our policy before I take down your information.' Crapshoot crossed his legs genteelly and watched her eye follow his hand down to the carnation which he propped up ever so gently before smiling engagingly.

'Fine.' Again the smile.

'Well, we *are* selective. And our selectivity requires

some basics, such as drawing your blood and assessing it for health risks, a personal questionnaire, a background check, return visits, things like that. Does that suit you?'

'Oh yes.' Crapshoot looked at the photo directly over her head. A father was showing his son how to fly-fish. The sun was dappled on their backs. The river ran through their legs. Both father and son had just cast. They waited patiently. It was a quiet scene. Crapshoot fiddled again with the carnation. 'What sorts of things do you check up on?'

'The mundane, the obvious. Like whether you're known to use drugs, have a criminal record, etcetera. Nothing that would surprise you or anyone. We just like to be sure.'

Crapshoot pointed to the photo. 'You see, those boys up there on your wall. They couldn't have a criminal record. You can just tell by looking at them. They're happy – a happy family.' He laughed.

Beth Sorensen didn't bother to turn. 'We're in the business of creating happy families. That's one of many we take credit for. Now if I can have your name.' She pulled out a white form and took a pen from a mug sitting atop the desk.

'Name?'

'Yes, name and occupation first. Then we'll leave some of the more sensitive questions to your written self-evaluation. So?' She looked up at Crapshoot.

He returned her gaze and thought for a moment, practising his intonation, readying himself for the new identity. 'Cornelius. Conan J. Cornelius.'

She started to write. Then looked up again. 'The poet?'

'I'm sorry?' He had not figured his part to be called on stage so quickly.

'Forgive me for asking, but are you the poet – the poet Conan Cornelius?'

Crapshoot watched her smile. Now more spontaneous, less professional. He too smiled. Broadly. 'Why, yes. Yes, indeed.' He recrossed his legs, this time the other way.

'That's fantastic. I'm sorry to call attention to it. We don't usually get people like you in here. That's all. I mean we get plenty of wonderful people. But ... this is an honour. I love your work. I read one of your poems just the other day. The one excerpted in the book review. The one called, what was it, "A Gelding's Pity", I think. I liked it very much.' She smiled again. And then contracted her brow in all seriousness. 'Did you intend that poem as a commentary on male–female relationships?'

Crapshoot smiled again. 'Well – '

She waved away his response. 'I'm sorry. Don't answer that. I know poets don't like to be asked dumb questions about what their poems mean. Forget I said that. I should really be more professional. This is only my second week.' She penned in the name, carefully and slowly, in the appointed space on her white sheet: *Conan J. Cornelius.*

'Oh, please. I'm well used to it. Poetry is a guessing game, you know.' He looked again at the photo. 'A guessing game that's always in season. You're free to ask whatever you want.'

Beth Sorensen blushed slightly and smiled again.

'OK?' He flashed his most solicitous smile.

'OK. Well, I'll leave you in privacy to answer these questions. Please remember to be completely candid, Mr Cornelius. We are extremely discreet with all information. Your privacy will in no way be compromised.'

'Thank you.' Crapshoot tilted his head, as a concerned donor would. 'How is it that my privacy is protected? I mean where is my name recorded, for example?'

'Oh, that's very secure. You needn't worry. You see that – ' She pointed with a painted red fingernail to the five-digit number at the top of the form – 'That's your code number. Only Dr Dotterweich, the clinic director, has the names and addresses that match those numbers. And he keeps them in his office in a locked cabinet. But that's the only place they exist. Out here and everywhere else, your sperm only go by number.'

'And the recipient, is that how you call it? How is her identity protected?'

'Oh, the same way. Her lab work is done by number. Only Dr Dotterweich has the real name in his files.' Beth Sorensen showed her professional concern with a strongly furrowed brow. 'Dr Dotterweich is very, very careful with confidentiality. Even the staff are not allowed in those files except under extraordinary circumstances,' she said obliquely. 'Dr Dotterweich keeps all the matches under lock and key on a master list. And that's where they stay.' She stood. 'I'll be right back. Please go ahead and start the paperwork.'

Crapshoot first noted his code number, committing it to his staunch memory. Then he turned to the extensive form: six pages, typed, with many empty lines available for each answer. He looked at the first question.

1. Describe your reasons for donating sperm. Please be frank and concise. Your response will be made available to clients to assist them in their selection of a donor.

Crapshoot tipped the pen against his lower lip. *Ahhhh.* So this was where the choice was made. If he were to write 'power' he could be perfectly frank – and absolutely concise. But being frank and concise seemed not so interesting. And in some ways, downright silly. The question solicited candour, but did it really want it? So many people always asked for candour with fingers crossed behind the back, not really wanting it. There was nothing magical about honesty. It was easy and direct. He thought of his grandfather's favourite saying: *If you always tell the truth, you have less to remember.* But then the question always rose nearly to his lips, the one that even as a young boy he'd often been tempted to ask in return: *If you had an excellent memory anyway, what advantage could the truth hold?* There was little advantage to the truth that he could see. Rarely was truth more interesting than lies. The truth was always two-dimensional – bland, nondescript, black and white. While the lies, well, were something beautiful – something to behold.

The truth had always made him feel deprived. But a good yarn, a story, a tall tale, or any of the same could flex and reactivate his mind. A classic con was the best of all fictions. Regular commerce was a dud: taxes, budgets, accounts payable and receivable, all the elements of a boring reality. But in the con game where Crapshoot resided, he was the sole profiteer. Nothing could take away his dominion. There were no rhythms, no ebbs and flows that constituted the normal business cycle. No, there was a glittering momentum that first halted and bucked and then exploded into his pocketbook and made him rich. Crapshoot hated the regular world, regular deals, regular jobs, regular money. Reality. Truth.

More importantly, the truth would not serve him well here. This would be his first and most important communication with that anonymous, quietly desperate soul who sat and waited for a baby. To pick him, she would need romance, poetry, a hope despite the hopeless. He was prepared. As Conan J. Cornelius, he could provide all these things and more. The seduction here was simple, more than any he had ever known. For in her not knowing him, he could be anything and anyone. He felt the gnawing and it inspired him. He *would* reel her in – now – with these words.

He poised the pen and wrote:

For poetry's sake.

There. That was certainly concise – and as frank as they could hope for. And it was destined to be effective.

He read it aloud: 'For poetry's sake.' He wasn't sure what he meant by it, but it had a nice ring to it. And it was less prosaic than *power*. He read it over and over again, much to his growing satisfaction.

11

'Come now!'
  'I am.'
  'I don't believe it!'
  'It's true.'
  'You *are* joking!'
  'I'm not.'
  'Well...'
  'Excuse me.'

Cocktail parties were like morgues, thought Caitlin, pouring another glass of Côtes-du-Rhône for the guests: so many people, so few worth talking to.

Serena caught up with her and grabbed her elbow: 'So when did you decide this?'

'Oh, so you believe it now?'

'Listen, honey, I think it's great. Pour me a little.' Serena cornered her and lowered her voice in an illusion of discretion. 'Will you have to actually get in bed with the guy or do they do it in a test tube?'

Caitlin poured the wine, not so inadvertently overflowing a few drops on to Serena's hand and white blouse sleeve.

'If there's a guy to fuck, Serena, don't worry. I'll let you in on it.'

In the entrance foyer, she spotted Paul. He was holding court with a few guests, a vodka on the rocks in one hand, a pedantic flourish in the other.

Back in the kitchen she went to work helping Rosita the Dominican maid arrange the spinach-wrapped oysters and the smoked trout on grilled bread. In Caitlin's realm of perfection the spinach had to be blanched exactly, the bread toasted the right amount. Food could always work out correctly with a little instinct, some patience, and a lot of money. The rules were so delineating and comforting. She catalogued her favourites in her head: cold oil in a hot pan, the ten-minute rule for basting, fingertips curled under when chopping. These were rules to live by. But they didn't make the larger issues of life any easier. She had once dared to imagine a perfect life with Paul. This cocktail party would have been a part of that. But when the guests were gone and Caitlin would be left with Rosita to clean up, there would be nothing left to distract – a bunch of cold rooms, cigarette butts in the toilet, nothing much to pass the setting of the sun.

'Can I help?' It was Annette, a Mayflower descendant from Darien. She was young for a divorcee but not for a mother. 'Serena told me. That's wonderful. I think any way that it can be done these days is a charm.'

'Thanks, Annette.' Caitlin handed the tray of oysters to Rosita to take into the living room. 'Here are the napkins. Watch the garnish.'

'I mean, look at me. I had my two and I regret not having more. Children are the stuff of life.' She lowered her voice. 'How will you pick the guy?'

'It's complicated.'

'Not nearly so complicated as the old method where the guy you were married to had to be the father of your kids too. I mean it.'

'It is complicated, believe me.'

'Oh yes. I don't doubt it. When I married Philip, you know, I was already – '

'I know. Pregnant.' Caitlin took out a bottle of mineral water from the refrigerator and poured a glass.

'Exactly. And I tell you, I was oblivious to the stares at the wedding.'

'But not everyone knew.'

'Of course not, silly. But I was proud. To have a child inside me. That was wonderful. A little something extra. When they grow up. That's a different story. I raised them well. But Tad is a rogue and scoundrel and can be mean as hell, just like his father. No, even worse than his father. Which, let me tell you, is saying a lot. And Cameron, oh God, young Cameron. Sometimes I think he needs more than the world has to offer him. Do you know what I mean?'

'Not really.' Caitlin tried to tidy up a bit in the kitchen with a dishtowel and a bottle of Windex, to tame the party's mess into reasonable suburban disarray – and more importantly, to stay away from the throng of guests for a few more minutes.

'And it's all chalked up to the fault of good soldiers like you and me. We march into motherhood with our trumpets blaring and our armour fully donned. And how does that armour serve us? It drowns us in the swamp of their adolescence. We're ill-equipped when you think about it.'

'Very dramatic, wouldn't you say?' Caitlin was wiping down the marble countertops. She'd heard Annette's good soldiers speech many times. The metaphor hadn't changed much over the years. Except that sometimes the parental knights drowned in a bog or a river instead of a swamp. Adolescence was always some body of water, though; and they, the mothers, were always drowned by their own armour.

'We're not given the right implements for dealing with it. I swear to you we're not. You'll see what I mean – when your child becomes a man or woman. They change. For the worst. It's a tragedy, really.

'Sometimes, when I see a child crossing the street in town, a young innocent child with no cares and no ugliness to him yet, I imagine what will happen in a few years: the earrings, the mohawk haircut, the drugs and the girls. God, it's even preppy to get an earring these days. I imagine the swamp of adolescence sucking in that poor kid – and then all of us. Sometimes I see Tad, and sometimes Cameron. And sometimes I just see myself. I mean, I wasn't really an angel either.' Annette laughed. Caitlin joined her. She was putting serving platters in the dishwasher. 'It's cruel somehow. People always look at dictators, tyrants, evil men and ask themselves *what kind of a child was that beast?* I think about that a lot. I mean even Mussolini was a child. When you try to picture that, it's odd. Not that many of our kids are going to end up as butchers. But still. It's tragic, really. If you look in any child's eyes, you see the beginnings of evil.'

This line attracted Caitlin's attention; unlike the others that had spurred her to clean more vigorously and listen less so. 'Really? How do you mean?'

'I mean, just look. It used to disturb me, actually, when I first had Tad. He was the cutest, cutest baby. He was gentle, a good boy. Cried very little. And such a healthy eater. But once when he was eight months or so and I had just taken him from the nanny and sent her on her night off and Philip had stayed at work late and we were all alone . . .'

Caitlin had closed the dishwasher and now stood at attention, drinking the mineral water and involved in Annette's story. 'Go on.'

'And I looked in his eyes.' Annette grew silent. Her face was quite pale.

'Yes?'

'And, like I say, I looked in his eyes. And, you know, one moment before they had been so cute and twinkling and full of love for me.'

'And?'

'And then when I looked again, they were empty.'

'What?'

'They were empty. There was no soul there. I swear there was no soul there. My baby had no soul.' Annette quickly dabbed a tear in the corner of her eye. Caitlin listened quietly and in horror. She felt a bit nauseous from tasting all the food and wine and then hearing this narration. But she had never seen Annette so sincere. 'And so, well, of course, I thought I was crazy for a moment, or something like that. And so I looked again and thank God there was the twinkling, back where it belonged. But the look on Tad's little face was a smile. And the smile seemed to say: *I can look the part of tender smiling baby, just watch.* And so I cried right there, while my baby smiled. And the more I cried, the more he smiled. I'd never felt so alone. The next day my shrink said it was stress from all the new responsibilities. Philip said I'd watched *Rosemary's Baby* too many times. Anyway, I never did hold Tad on my lap or look him directly in the eye after that. I just couldn't.'

'That's horrible.'

Annette looked startled and changed gear, haughtily walking over to the fridge and helping herself to mineral water. 'Christ. It's not horrible,' she said embarrassed at her candour. 'It's motherhood. You'll see, dammit. It's the way things are. It's not very strange really, when you think about it.'

'I'm sorry.'

'Listen to my complaining. Blast that wine, Caitlin, where are you hiding your Scotch?'

Caitlin motioned to the living room and Annette was on her way.

'Well, if it isn't – ' Paul came in the other end of the kitchen, well drunk by now, one shirt tail out, the vodka tumbler empty, cradled by his limp wrist in the gulch between his shoulder and left pectoral, a solitary lime wedge sliding viscously along its base like a puck on ice. His face was mean, slack at the mouth from drink, contorted at the forehead from anger. ' – if it isn't the future bionic mother and her two healthy ovaries!'

'Paul, sit down.' Caitlin fished in the cupboard for a box of crackers and poured some in a bowl. 'Here, eat something.'

'No, I don't wanna. I want to ask you – if it's you who's been telling – I mean why – ' He wagged his free forefinger ostensibly in the direction of Caitlin but it ended up rebuking the floor. 'Why, that is, why exactly, that I am a freak without – ' The tumbler fell to the floor, cracking into four or five neat pieces. The lime sputtered across the linoleum. 'Look at that. Can't even hold my liquor.' Paul laughed and stooped uncertainly to try to collect the glass.

'Leave it. I'll get it,' said Caitlin, going into the pantry to retrieve the broom and dustpan, fuming and pinching herself for having confided in someone like Serena.

'Oh no – I'm good for something.' When she got back, there was blood on his hand and a smirk on his face.

'I'm taking you upstairs.'

*

MISBEGOTTEN

In the dark bedroom like a womb Caitlin pulled the covers over Paul and worked to clean the gash. It was a good half an inch long and deep enough to keep bleeding. She cleaned it out with hydrogen peroxide and then gently wrapped it in a thin piece of gauze while he moaned terribly with the alcohol and the discomfort. Then she slipped off his socks and loafers and sat by his side. Soon he was alert to her and staring. His eyes were blue, steady, their ready clarity dulled slightly by the vodka.

'I want you.' He groped at her with his healthy hand and ripped her blouse slightly.

'Stop. Sleep.'

He bolted. In the tumble of his efforts they both fell to the floor and the gauze slipped off. Caitlin tasted blood in her mouth and the covers cascaded on to them both. He rolled on top of her, binding her to the Berber carpet. Paul worked clumsily and painfully to undress her, cursing repeatedly and thrashing like a salmon in an attempt to throw his trousers past his knees. Unable to unhook her bra, he pulled at the strap and yanked one of the cups down so that it wedged against her flesh like a third unhappy breast. Then he went to work on her underwear, pulling sideways in a futile manipulation. Giving up, he pulled off his own and with less success tried to force himself inside her. He pressed with a maddening concentration and she was aware of his panting under the strain. And of the sound of guests leaving downstairs. After a moment the breathing was steadier and she realised he was asleep. She slid him off to the side and placed a pillow under his head and the covers along the length of his half-naked body.

While Paul snored, she re-wrapped the gauze and thought of her child.

12

Crapshoot walked into the taxi stand on Barrow, thinking of pyramids.

Having just stopped by the post office, he dumped the week's collection on to his desk. Later, he would separate out the phoney invoice cheques in order to mail them to a bank in Delaware. Meanwhile, he sat down to contemplate a new pyramid scam. With typewriter fully loaded, Crapshoot sat down to compose:

Dear Madam/Sir:

It will hardly surprise you to hear that your personal Catalyst Investments Counsellor, after careful research and risk assessment, has chosen a new series of wise and dynamic investment choices for your portfolio. As in the past, these selections are picked by our unique and patented algorithmic investment selection program which, in its five-year history, has seen an average return 8% better than the S&P 500 Index.

Due to the selective and exclusive nature of this investment, minimum payments are ordinarily restricted to $500. However, due to your good relationship with our firm, this minimum is temporarily being waived so that you may contribute as little as $200 to your initial investment.

> Instructions are enclosed. Thank you for your continued confidence.
>
> Best wishes,
>
> R. K. Thayer-Bock III
> Vice-President, Private Investment Division

Crapshoot triumphantly pulled the letter out of the typewriter and loaded the rickety small Xerox machine in the corner with many sheets of a generic-looking black letterhead that read PYRAMID CORPORATION. Over the past year, Pyramid Corporation had been many different things to many different people. In late May, with the days growing longer, it had been a start-up biotech company soliciting money from venture capital firms; in August, in the stultifying heat of those dog days, it had mutated into a small consultancy specialising in advice on getting new products into emerging Russian markets; in December, as tinsel went up and the first snow came down, it had imported itself into an employment agency promising to find work for prospective applicants in exchange for a modest $50 application fee; and now, in February, as the snow turned permanent, it had found itself new and gainful occupation as an investment brokerage. Within a matter of weeks, as the thaw arrived, it would have to reinvest the proceeds and, bullish on itself, would bond itself to some other stock and trade.

Crapshoot set about signing the copied letters, still warm with the thrill of Xeroxed duplicity, in a lofty hand where the T in Thayer rose up in dramatic strokes and nearly usurped the place of the hyphen. Then he retrieved from his briefcase a bunch of official-looking prospectuses he had collected by writing to different brokerages, an instruction sheet, additional and equally irrelevant but impressive-looking financial documents printed in small black type, and collated the whole collection. Each packet he folded and placed into dignified pre-stamped envelopes inscribed with the understated Pyramid Corporation logo and one of his recent postbox addresses. After licking and sealing the mailings with a self-satisfied thwack of his palm, he put them aside for later addressing with names selected from middle-class suburban area phone books in California.

He counted one hundred and five solicitations. Based on his experience that would yield approximately one to two sucker cheques. In the next few days he would send out hundreds more similar mailings, boosting the total return. Crapshoot would then take the financing from the later mailings and mail cheques to the earlier customers with congratulatory letters exalting the amazing and gratifying 100 per cent three-month return on their investment and exhorting them to quickly send in more equity, in order to take advantage of booming returns. Weeks later he would repeat the process, but the second letter of congratulations would state that due to unprecedented recent demand, the minimum investment was being raised significantly – to $5000. The letter, in whispered and earnest tones, insisted that though it knew this was a large amount for the average investor, the firm was certain that returns would continue in their swashbucklingly happy ways. Clients were urged to act quickly. Crapshoot would always score big on this round. Many investors would balk at this hefty minimum; some, newly suspicious, would also decline to reply. But one old pensioner would always send in her life savings – anywhere from $5000, or on a good day, upwards of $25000. And then Crapshoot would make a speedy exit from the brokerage business: close out the bank accounts and the post office box, and move on to new pursuits.

Crapshoot reread the original letter and admired its simple, crafty eloquence: the ingenious indications that Pyramid Corporation had somehow done business with the party before, or in any case that the party had somehow and fortunately ended up on their private client mailing list; the obligatory sop to the fictional customer's fictionally good fictional relationship with the correspondingly fictional firm; the tactful way the minimum investment was addressed; and, finally, the grandness of the sign-off, complete on each copy with the flourish of penmanship that graced the Thayer-Bock name, a perfect aristocratic hybrid of Boston Brahmin and Dutch ancestry designed to inspire blind faith in every investor.

'More love letters, Billy?'

'Of course.'

The dispatcher was taking a break, sucking coffee out of Styrofoam and spinning lazily around in his oversized vinyl desk chair.

'To who, Billy? You got no lovers.' A chuckle.

'Deals, you know,' said Crapshoot quietly, adjusting his carnation.

'I know, business. Tell me about it. Like these fucking drivers today. I tell them there's nothing, 'cause there's nothing. Not 'cause I have any reason. What else? Then when I get a call in and try to get out the job, I get lip from that motherfuckin' Haitian bastard Toby who doesn't even know his way to the train station. And then, would you believe it, Romeo gets a flat on the fucking Merritt on his way to the call? I tell you, Billy, whatever it is, isn't. And whatever it isn't, it is. Got me?'

'I'll see you.'

'Wanna work tonight? It'll be good later.'

'No.'

'Oh, well, I guess you're flush. When was the last you worked a shift anyway?'

'A week and two days.'

'Right. See ya.'

Crapshoot nodded.

As he was passing out the door, the dispatcher grabbed Crapshoot's elbow with a small hand. 'The rent?'

Crapshoot took out a money roll and pulled out two twenties and tossed them on the dispatcher's desk. Then he carefully wiped his elbow: 'Don't grab me.'

The dispatcher smiled, then stopped nervously. They stared at each other for a moment, quite serious, until Crapshoot grinned, his broad, generous grin. 'I'll be seeing you. Don't look so grim.'

It was a sunny day despite the cold. Crapshoot buttoned up his overcoat to the neck as he stepped out on to the street. He mailed the stack of letters at the nearest postbox and fished for his own mail in the briefcase. At the Dunkin' Donuts he took a window table and sat down to open it: six cheques from retailers to whom he'd addressed phoney invoices only weeks ago; a birthday card from his mother five days late; a small note that had arrived at his PO box in Stamford, typed on grand heavy bond stationery with a logo at the top that read:

Inseminology Institute
'The Best Beginnings'

Mr Conan J. Cornelius
PO Box 1657
Stamford, Connecticut 09871

Dear Mr Cornelius,

We are delighted to have you as a donor in our program. It is because of generous sponsors like yourself that the Inseminology Institute is able to offer loving families the opportunity to have the gift of children.

We are honoured to have a donor of your eminent esteem in our program. Our efforts are directed at getting the best quality applicants like yourself so that the next generation is a happy, talented and productive one.

Rest assured that we will protect your privacy and anonymity with the utmost attention and discretion. Please call if you have any question whatsoever.

Best wishes,

Richard Dotterweich, MD, PhD
Clinic Director

Crapshoot finished his coffee and sent the letter into the trash along with the cup. *Well, well. Conan J. Cornelius.* He liked the name. It was distinguished, haughty and sophisticated – yet masculine, unusual and rhythmic – a good name for his poetic self. He was becoming inspired to write a poem or two, in fact. It would be no difficult task. He had always fancied himself an artist – certainly a genius. Just a pen and paper. What a simple life that could be, he thought. *What a simple life, indeed.*

13

The idea of having a baby – without Paul, with another – grew on her. It had an appeal as revenge. And no one could say he didn't deserve a little vengeance. Yes, a baby without him was what she wanted anyway. A baby with someone else. Angry at herself, Caitlin remembered that first anniversary evening in Miami – that evening and the weak idiocy with which she first wanted a baby.

On South Beach, with the sun, the moon, the shimmering water and the girls, Paul had looked at only the girls.

They walked down that Miami strip, where the sand meets the chic restaurants and the bars are open until three; where the neon mates with art deco and conceives glitz. There, amongst the models and the Cubans, the Hassids and the retirees, they walked. But it was mainly the models that remained in Caitlin's mind.

The place seemed suspended in the pastel haze of a permanent fashion shoot. Girls, eighteen, twenty, with European exquisiteness in the face and serious figures that made every male pivot for a view. Including Paul.

Caitlin noticed he had been trying to keep a straight face, to deadpan the tremendous opportunities at every angle. She had waited, chuckling inside herself, ready for his weakness to kick in. And when it had, she was there with a camera-like memory to file it away.

It was a blonde, predictably, with legs up to the ozone, a pert smile, *very* pert breasts and an at once flirtatious and cold stare that made Caitlin's skin crawl. She looked at Paul from a half-block away and Paul was barely able to control himself. He tripped on the pavement, then tried to squelch the embarrassment by clearing his throat, ended up with spittle on his lip which he then removed with his linen sleeve, finally sneezing on same sleeve and shaking his head in frustration.

'What's wrong, honey?' asked Caitlin, with her best smile.

'Nothing. The air. It's chilly.'

'It's eighty degrees.'

'Yes, but the breezes.'

'Tropical.'

'Right. How about a drink?'

A drink. That sounded like a good idea. A margarita to freeze the throat.

In the nearest art deco hotel bar, on the purple cushioned stools, with no sign of the sounds of the ocean and loud mambo music from the speakers, they tried to talk. But the noise was deafening and Paul took to casting lazily about with his eyes for more opportunities. They came from all sides, in all colours, in all nationalities, but with only one shape – model-slender.

South Miami Beach had built itself into a modelling mecca, and photographers came from all over the world to photograph these perfect, statuesque symbols of all that was good and exciting in America.

Caitlin tried taking Paul's hand in hers but that only seemed, like a joystick on a video game, to initiate far greater movement and activity.

'What are you looking for?' she finally asked.

'The waiter.'

'Which one? The one in the six-inch miniskirt or the one with the dyed blonde hair?'

'The one with the check,' he said gruffly, after coughing once.

It occurred to Caitlin that the whole flavour of South Beach was sex. If you looked at the menu, the swordfish was seasoned with cilantro, the salmon with ginger, the tuna steak with lime. But the unstated speciality of the house was sex – as a side dish, appetiser or dessert. Not that there was anything wrong with that. But it would have been nice for Caitlin to experience it. Sex was everywhere. Certainly on the beach, where models tended their immaculate complexions under umbrellas and feigned nonchalance. Or in the bars, where sex lingered, strapped into spandex and roller blades, in locomotion, looking for something or someone. Or in the hotel rooms, where every manner of everything was surely going on.

Caitlin had looked at herself in the mirror that morning after four sunny days. The tan lines had begun to grace her like a new paint job and her skin looked supple – wonderful. *Why did Paul not appreciate it?* She looked good, she thought. Not great, but good. Or maybe not.

Sex was everywhere – on South Beach.

She didn't feel a part of it. Not that she wanted that exactly. Hardly. The sordidness of it did not impress her. The posing. The flirtation. It was truly unbecoming.

But sex was everywhere.

Paul had tapped into the energy and this left her alone. She did not want the stares of the men gawking at anything that inadvertently swayed a hip in their direction. She just wanted Paul's attention. For at least a moment.

And sex was everywhere.

When a young girl passed, Paul couldn't help tossing looks over his shoulder – ever so occasionally – to check the perspective. Caitlin caught him each time. And he covered his tracks sheepishly, commenting on the beach front renovations and the boutiques.

But there had to be more to it all than sex.

'Are you aware of the poetry around you?' Caitlin had asked finally.

'What?'

'I mean that girl had a cute butt, but do you think she's aware of the poetry of all things?'

'How do you mean?'

Again a gaggle of distractions passed to the left. Then to the right.

'I mean *that*. Is it just their looks? Or do you really want to get to know them?'

'Caitlin, I can't help looking. It doesn't mean anything.' They had stopped to look in at the window of a jeweller's boutique. Gold watchbands. Sparkling gems. Glitter. More objects of desire. Very tempting – and expensive. Like everything else in South Beach.

'What could they offer you? *Really?*'

'What the hell are you talking about? I'm not planning anything. They're not *offering* anything. These girls are high-paid supermodels. They couldn't give a damn about *me* – or you.'

'That's not what I'm asking. I want to know if they offered, what would the offer consist of?'

Paul shook his head in frustration. 'I have no idea what you're talking about. Listen, should we get back to the hotel or do you want a nightcap?'

So Paul had no conception of the poetry of all things

either. One year of marriage and no sense of the importance of it all. Looking in at the shop window at the jewels and the gold, Caitlin swallowed hard on the air that escaped as her heart fell.

'I want a baby.'

Paul turned to her. 'What?'

'A baby. That's what I want.'

Paul smiled awkwardly. 'How about a diamond bracelet instead?'

Caitlin twisted the diamond bracelet at the compliment. 'Thank you. My husband bought it for me as a first anniversary present.'

'I'm not exaggerating. It *is* one of the most gorgeous ones I've ever seen. Just *gorgeous*. He clearly loves you very much.'

'He's just rich,' Caitlin smiled.

'Hey, don't knock that,' said the secretary.

'Hey. Does it look as though I do?' Caitlin flashed the full expanse of her jewelleried hands. Many carats. Many, many sparkles. 'He is rich. But he's a fool really. A rich fool, but a fool. And I feel sorry for him.'

The secretary looked away embarrassedly. 'I'll ring the doctor and tell him you're here. Do you have an appointment?'

Caitlin shook her head.

Dotterweich smiled mechanically as she entered the office. 'Something to tell me?'

'Yes, I've chosen my man.'

Dotterweich smiled again. 'That's very good. Now, do you know the task at hand? You go home and sleep. You let this choice percolate within your being – let it settle into your neural pathways. And then you wake up and see if you feel the same way. And then, if you do, you come here again tomorrow and tell me. Nature needs time and this is the least you can do for nature. Sleep on it.'

Caitlin felt a stab of impatience but appreciated the doctor's caution. It sounded like good advice. 'I'm not going to change my mind,' she said, testing.

'I know. Sleep on it anyway.'

Sleep on it, she thought as she left the office. It occurred to her that she had already been asleep a long time.

14

Crapshoot did not like libraries.

The stifling quiet of so many books, so many of them ceaselessly unread, weighed on him. The public libraries were the worst, he thought, with their clientele of retirees and the homeless, their sixties furniture and stale odour. The lack of life and commerce in libraries bored him. There was no action. It was a place where people lived their lives through the pages of a magazine or the spine of a bestseller. He didn't respect any of it. Not the card catalogues with their self-righteous and intimidating expansiveness, not the old librarian volunteers with their earnest helpful advice, nor the squeak of shoes along the linoleum tiles of the stacks, nor the tired and frustrated feeling that he felt when he actually had to try to find something there.

He had at least come to the Westbridge branch. He figured it would have a better collection than Northport's, which had been closed all days except two due to budget cuts.

'Excuse me, would you be kind enough to tell me where I might find a collection of the poetry of Conan J. Cornelius?' he asked in a library whisper. The reference librarian was sitting behind her desk, studiously peeling a banana.

She looked over her reading glasses at the well-dressed man with a broad grin, such a polite manner, a lovely carnation a-pocket, and the obvious interest in poetry. She decided he was worthy of her best reference efforts. She put aside the banana on a napkin and stood.

'Well, that would be simple,' she responded as she came around the side of her desk to start looking in the card catalogues. Crapshoot stepped back with relief at her eagerness to find the book for him. He hated to be left on his own to do that sort of thing. 'We merely look in the authors' catalogue here under ... what did you say that poet's name was?'

'Cornelius is the name. Conan J. Cornelius,' he said quietly.

'Contemporary?'

Crapshoot thought for a moment, surprised by the question. 'Yes.'

'Ah, yes. Beckett. Benson, hmmm, Canterbury, Cummings, oh gee, hmmm, here it is ... Cornelius, Conan J. Let's see now. We only have one collection of his poetry, a book titled *Up the Fallow Hill*. Is this the one you're interested in?'

'That will do nicely.'

The librarian led him to a small alcove off the main reading room. After a quick search, she pulled out a thin green hardback volume with the customary cellophane library wrap and handed it to him. 'Enjoy.' She smiled.

'Thank you,' he smiled back.

He turned over the volume. There was a very small black and white headshot of a distinguished-looking man wearing glasses and leaning against what looked to be a tree. It was unmistakably the same man who had hailed his cab not long ago. Crapshoot read the back cover.

MISBEGOTTEN

> *In this, his fourth volume of poems, Conan J. Cornelius explores his familiar preoccupations – loss, infidelity, elusive loyalties and spiritual rebirth – in his characteristically unique and haunting lyric.*

And the blurb of a review on the front cover:

> *The harbinger of new poetic imaginings, a genius as constant as it is daring, the verse of Cornelius, boldly reminiscent of Gerard Manley Hopkins and Dylan Thomas, offers thirsty souls the potion for literary redemption.*
>
> *– **The Sun Literary Supplement***

There was no biography.

Crapshoot sat stiffly at one of the library tables and scanned the names of the poems on the contents page. He flipped to the poem that had offered the title:

> *Up the fallow hill*
> *I went*
> *With not the belt of reason at my back.*
> *Imagining growth, so sickly and infernal*
> *Aside, apart, awash – with me.*
> *In Homer I did not find the way that told me what*
> *And so, the fallow hill did hold me.*
> *Forced gazing, forest grazing, parts of me unwind.*
> *You can look too, he'd said. I took him at his*
> *Word.*
> *God had not handed me it either as I looked upon*
> *The fallow hill.*
> *Up the fallow hill I went to find what was once*
> *Mine.*

Don't!
And so I didn't
Until temerity did cling to me.
Up the fallow hill, I said.
Growth, apart, aside – instead.

Crapshoot sat bewildered. The poem made no sense to him at all. It had hardly been recognisable as a poem except for the occasional rhymes and the placement of the lines, one above the other in jagged permanence upon the page. He reread various parts, whispered them to himself. *A genius as constant as it is daring.* He discerned no genius lurking in those lines. It angered him deeply that such idiotic ramblings could be erroneously referred to as genius. But suddenly he laughed. Of course.

A con job.

He had to admire the extent of the con: so many pages, bound together in an acclaimed volume – one which had sold for $12.95 and had garnered such eager praise. It was suddenly gratifying to see such a far-flung and unusual example of his world view right here in the library. It had never occurred to him – a poetry con. He laughed again. Very clever. He would have to investigate. Balancing the book delicately in his left palm, as though to measure its weight, he wondered how many copies had been sold. Certainly every library, every university had a copy. What was the profit margin? Uncomfortably small, probably. But it was still admirable. Such brazen con artistry. And he had picked Cornelius's pocket, not even realising that the man was in turn picking the world's!

He chose to sample another poem with a title that intrigued him in its quackery, 'Motion in Motion'. That was perfect. True jacking off, he thought:

MISBEGOTTEN

Motion in Motion
Is.
What else can we say about that tautology?
I have not found motion any other way
Except in rooms upstairs, down, within, out
In my old home on the old street
Where mother was sold.
Why did I sell her? You ask until told.
Emboldened I was I tell you that.
She fetched quite the price at market.
Mark it!
She begged not to be.
But markets are markets, the tax man, what glee!
Motion in motion,
With or with me.

Again, more briefly, the tide of a horrible confusion drowned him. But again he laughed when he was satisfied at the recurring absurdity of each line. Such brazen disregard for meaning, he thought, as he looked at the lines again. It was charming.

Commerce lived even here – in the library.

'May I check this out, please?' he asked at the circulation desk, with the grandest of smiles.

'I'm sorry, this is from our reference section. It doesn't circulate.'

'Oh that's a shame,' he said.

In the bathroom he removed the small electromagnetic strip by ripping it off the flyleaf. Then he adjusted the book between the taut waist of his pants and belt and his firm lower back. He replaced his jacket and overcoat, propped up the carnation, slicked back his hair, unlocked the bathroom door and left.

He walked confidently past the circulation desk, through the metal detector and outside into the chilly morning air. He'd returned the reference librarian's wave.

Cons big and small. He got into his cab and drove off.

15

'This one.'

Dotterweich glanced down at the portfolio Caitlin had handed him. 'This one?'

'Yes.'

'A wise choice.' Dotterweich scanned the papers, mumbling softly to himself.

'When do we get started?'

'Oh, quite soon. We have donations on hand. We will have to do some preliminary chemical and DNA analyses – and then ... well – ' Dotterweich extended his huge hand across the desk to cover Caitlin's. 'We will make a baby.' He laughed. In the thickness of his European accent, the process sounded warm, hopeful, easy. 'What, may I ask, attracted you especially to *this* profile?'

It had only been a random phrase, Caitlin knew. But she was loath to admit it, especially to this doyen of the scientific frontier. She recalled looking over the last batch of profiles in the den the night before. Paul had paid no attention. Lately he'd been unconcerned with the process. *You're the one getting knocked up, you pick it*, he said as he left for work one day. Ever since Dotterweich's harangues, his resentment was unyielding.

As midnight approached, she spread the new profiles on the carpet, as though to line her suitors at her feet. One after another, she read the minimal information in hopes of gleaning a flicker of paternal perfection. How to choose a father from such things as occupation, weight and cholesterol count? She considered tossing them down the staircase and seeing which carried farthest. Again she consulted the limited information before her. One friend suggested doing an exhaustive astrological analysis of each one. Another offered palmistry. Those were as good options as any, she knew. But which one? Even if you're willing to abandon yourself to the fringes of a faith, you have to know which faith to choose.

Could she leave this decision to fate, to luck – to God? No, too important.

What she knew she needed was some inspiration. She had been astonished at the stupidity of profile after profile. People had so little to offer. For inspiration, she looked to one of the most probing questions on the application: *Describe your reasons for donating sperm. Please be frank and concise.* The answers were varied but nonetheless boring:

I love children.

Hardly an explanation of why he would want to donate his potential children to someone else.

For the advancement of science. Science is the new frontier. I want to be a part of this research.

So clinical. It sounded like a lecture from Dotterweich. Maybe it *was* Dotterweich. No doubt the old man had wanked into a cup at some point. It would save him a few bucks.

MISBEGOTTEN

To make money.

At least that was honest. Perhaps, the truest of all. But did she want those to be the three words she took with her home to baby?

To do something worthy with my life.

Too pathetic.

To please God. To join the kingdom of heaven.

Too fanatical.

I want to help others, and help myself at the same time. I would like to give the gift of life to a mother who could not otherwise experience it. I am sensitive to the concerns of parents and children alike. [There was an arrow and the response continued on the back of the page.] *There is something sad about a couple who would like to have a child in the household but cannot. I would like to help that couple. It's terrible that God granted some the right to have children and not others. I'm trying to balance things out. I think I'm a better man for it. In fact, I know I'm a better man for it.*

Besides being longwinded and ridiculous, this didn't follow the directions, which said to be concise. Couldn't be too bright. Forget it.

This was the last batch. If Daddy wasn't here, then Daddy wasn't anywhere. But what was she really looking for? What did she expect that someone could say in a silly questionnaire that would be profound? Perhaps she should just go ahead and allow Dotterweich to make the match based on purely biological criteria. He'd offered, even pressured to do that many times, but she insisted on having ultimate control. In many ways a biological decision appealed to her. A eugenic approach to her child, why not? She did want the healthiest, the smartest, the loveliest – the best behaved. What parent wouldn't? It was a natural desire. Yet Dotterweich's diligence, his dossiers – his Darwinian determination – had deterred her. There had to be an inkling, perhaps just a vapour of something she could distil from those limited answers.

She started on the new pile. She selected one at random.

Again, the question: *Describe your reasons for donating sperm. Please be frank and concise.*

The answer genuinely surprised her:

For poetry's sake.

That was interesting. What exactly did it mean? She wasn't sure, but she immediately took a liking to it. Yes, *for poetry's sake*. That would have to be why. The answer was at once mysterious, mystical and spiritual. And genuinely profound. Why hadn't she herself seen it before? There was an essential poetry to all of this process. Without it, there was no purpose. Nothing. Poetry. Yes. That was the purpose.

Caitlin immediately turned to the other parts of the profile. *Profession: Poet*. Well, hardly surprising. The physical superficials looked ordinary, acceptable. *Religion: Catholic*. So what. That had never mattered to her one way or the other. So this was to be the father of her children – a Catholic poet. Perhaps, an Irish one. Her heart danced at the romance of it.

She ran upstairs to tell Paul, but then decided against it.

MISBEGOTTEN

He would only resent her enthusiasm. She didn't sleep that night, waiting for dawn to call Dotterweich.

'One phrase.'
'One phrase?'
'Only one.'
'Which, may I ask?'
'Where he gives his reason for donating sperm – he says, *For poetry's sake.*'

Dotterweich frowned and looked again at the profile.

'I see. Yes. That's very good.' Dotterweich looked at the profile again and frowned slightly.

'Is something wrong?' Caitlin asked.

As Caitlin sat in the chair across from him, Dotterweich got up and headed for the files. Although he was sufficiently happy with the choice, he didn't approve of her reason. No, not at all. *For poetry's sake.* How could that answer inform a logical decision? Perhaps he should remove such an open-ended question from the questionnaire entirely. The response was useless for evaluation – utterly unscientific. He had only included it as a concession to clients who desired that type of emotional affiliation with the donor.

But this particular response worried him. *For poetry's sake.* The flipness of those words, the hollow cadence of intelligence devoid of scientific discipline. He shook his head gently. He had predicted that Caitlin Bourke would make the decision with such characteristic imbalance. He had campaigned vigorously for the right to make the match based on purely genetic proclivities. But Caitlin Bourke had been determined. Dotterweich opened the locked file drawer and retrieved the coded listing that linked each donor number with a real name and address.

After locating the number of the profile Caitlin Bourke had selected, he scanned across the page: *Conan J. Cornelius*. Yes, of course. Now he remembered the name. A staff member had referred to him as a famous poet. Dotterweich had sent Cornelius a letter assuring him of privacy. Well, perhaps this wasn't so bad. A poet, after all, should be permitted such a response. And Cornelius was apparently a poet of some renown. Good genetic stock of a type.

He replaced the file and turned back to Caitlin who was staring at him, awaiting a reply. He could see the worry in her eyes. She wasn't getting enough sleep. He had better be careful: there was no need to alarm a client. 'By all accounts, you've made an excellent choice. This donor, I think I can say it safely enough without jeopardising his anonymity,' he lowered his voice to disclose the secret, 'is a very well-regarded poet. A man of not little acclaim. A talent. And very sophisticated. I believe he teaches at a prestigious university,' he added without basis, feeling that an occasional white lie to heighten the confidence of a client was allowable. 'This donor is of excellent stock. We have screened him very carefully. You have nothing to fear. He is a true intellect and artist.'

'I'm happy to hear that. I thought you were disturbed at first.'

'Not at all.'

'Now what?'

'I'll take care of the preliminary lab work. And then we'll be in touch.' He smiled.

'Then I'll look forward to hearing from you.'

When she was gone, Dotterweich looked out the window. The trees bowed under winter. It had snowed again that afternoon and three fresh inches clung to the frozen grasses and the icy river beds. Already, it was a record winter for precipitation. The world was testing its inhabitants, thought Dotterweich. This season, every creature, large and small, was being naturally selected for an ability to withstand the cold. He imagined the bears a hundred miles north-west burrowed into the cleavage of the hillsides in wintry hibernation. He so admired the concept. What an adaptation it was to remove oneself from the world entirely, to slow down all metabolic functions so as to nearly not exist. Brilliant. Mother nature was brilliant. Humans, too, would do well to follow the bears. He closed his eyes and imagined the isolation of a snowy hillside. *For poetry's sake*, he thought again. It struck him as a crude way of thinking. Typically human, typically self-destructive. Dangerous. People would do well to learn something from nature, the only true poet. As a piece of him remained in the world, troubled by this human consideration, the rest of him breathed deeply in the slow rhythm of an imagined hibernation.

16

Never had he thought it could be so hard.

Crapshoot bowed his head over the paper and cursed. Then he poised the pen and started anew:

The bond is clear
In this insemination
The time is near
For this

Christ. It *was* hard. He referred again to *Up the Fallow Hill* and then glanced hopefully at the thesaurus at his elbow. Something would come his way. The trick was not to take it so seriously, to imagine himself Cornelius, to con the words out of himself. But the trick was to communicate the message he needed to communicate. *That* was something the real Cornelius hadn't had to deal with.

'Wanna work, Billy?'

Crapshoot didn't answer. He was on the verge of a good rhyme.

'Do ya?'

Jesus, he'd lost it. 'What?'

'Work? You want it? Cato's sick and Mark's on a job to Foxwoods.'

'No thank you.'

'What's up. Love letters?'

Crapshoot smiled. 'No. Love poems.'

The dispatcher guffawed. 'Go to it, Billy.'

Perhaps the trick was not to worry about rhyme. It was much easier that way. Clearly, Cornelius didn't really worry about it. But Crapshoot was used to visualising a problem and tackling it quickly. This was proving all too frustrating.

He consulted the thesaurus again, searching for synonyms of *insemination*. There weren't any.

Poetry was obviously a hoax. Of that he was sure. But why was it so difficult to get a few lines on paper? *What a honeysuckle mess.* What an unprofitable enterprise. He imagined Cornelius slaving away over pages and pages. And then all that you got was a paltry little book. Crapshoot rifled through the pages with disdain. Such silliness. He'd heard the government funded things like this. Silly. He would have to tap into that somehow.

It was important to keep the purpose at hand. A beautiful poem? For that he didn't really give a damn. What he wanted instead was a beautiful con – means to an end – words only for what they could accomplish in the real world.

The con would be about ownership. He wanted to own her – whoever she would be – and her child. He imagined her lonely, desperate, clutching to her great last hope. He remembered dully the stories of his own mother who had desperately tried to have him for years with a biblical tenacity. She had cried every night at the hope of it. And then finally one day, he'd emerged: nothing close to what she had imagined.

He imagined blissfully how lonely a woman in need of a child could be. And necessarily her husband had failed her. That's why she was going up the turnpike, all the way to the sperm bank, all the way to find her child. With some real sperm that could do the job. It excited him to think of inseminating her through the anonymity of a lab vial.

He could own her. And her child. By fathering her child he could own the both of them. But it had to be done right. With the right words. With the right poems. With the right identity.

The excitement started to grip him. The feeling gnawed at his heart, right below the carnation. His hand drifted down to the linen over his crotch, under which he could feel his erection growing and growing. He massaged it surreptitiously.

'You sure you don't wanna work, Billy?'

Crapshoot arched his back and glared at the dispatcher. 'I said, I'm busy.'

The dispatcher suppressed the chuckle he had coming and went back to his radio.

Crapshoot felt something brewing. He crossed out what he'd written, closed his eyes briefly to clear his mind, and poised the pen again:

For poetry's sake
A spot in time
Not for money, or love, or any part of flesh.

He looked at the new lines. Now that was the type of thing. They had written themselves. He hadn't thought about it. He reread them, slowly at first, then over and over, faster and faster. Not bad, he thought. They did say something. And they were his. What's more, they felt like poetry. He was proud of them. They were suitably mysterious: at once nonsensical, at once perfectly clear. Pure poetry.

Crapshoot laughed. He had always felt that he was a born poet. Now it was clear. What a con, he thought. There was something equally grand about every role. As a taxi driver, he was no less anything than as a poet. And as a businessman he was entirely the same. The world was his, of that he was sure.

I am always in season.

17

Slight shifts in the topography lead to a wholly different landscape. When a house is built on a hillside where there had been nothing but trees, there is a change that's bigger than the house itself. When a beach dune washes away, leaving only traces of itself, a view from afar puts together a different picture that might proclaim less than beach. Small details can make big drama. Potent medicines come in minute doses. Scientists have struggled with the possibility that the smaller the dose, in fact, the greater the potency. So believe the homoeopaths. In healing, as in all things, a little means a lot.

It is part of changing seasons that signals here and there tell you that soon the world will be an entirely different place: the groundhog spies his shadow, the ground smells robust – a piece of ice breaks away and floats downstream.

On this March day, where spring hinted at itself with the sun, Caitlin Bourke knew that by small degrees, that sun would be magical. For today she slipped out the door in an erstwhile uncharacteristic state, a state signalled merely by small changes in chemicals, tiny bodily processes, infinitesimal alchemies of still more runtish scale. That morning, upon waking, she noticed no change in her physique. But her mood had shifted like a California fault line. And she felt happy – even joyous.

She was pregnant.

Though she imagined the baby inside her, she knew it was only a possibility, not a being. But, in her heart of hearts, she knew she'd conceived. There was something different. Something hormonal. There was no doubt about it.

She was pregnant.

Though she felt the heaviness and sensitivity of her breasts that normally signalled her oncoming menstruation, the slight nausea that inexplicably came on with the shadow of hunger heralded something else.

She was pregnant.

Days before, Dotterweich had told her to expect the worst. The technician gave her a sedative and the semen sample was implanted. In its clinical style it was undramatic. The procedure took a short time. On the way home, even then, an hour later, she knew she was pregnant. Paul drove her home. He smiled the whole way, bravely. She held his hand to encourage him. It was easy to be generous, for she felt happiness growing inside her, an emotion unexpected, surprising her to the core.

Pregnancy, something she had always dreamed of, surprised her when it came. Not with its timing – she expected that – but with its simultaneous smallness and hugeness. There, all of a sudden, in her belly, was nothing but everything; a dot but a world; a prayer but a deliverance. Lodged in the blood-engorged lining of her uterus, feasting on nourishment sent by many vessels, was a fertilised egg: not even anything but everything anyway.

When that morning she felt the sensations that caused her to go outside and feel the subtle warming of the air, she forgot her jacket and walked joyously through the snow. The thought that now she was responsible for two beings spun her along to the road. There she prayed.

Paul sounded pleased when she called and told him the good news. His resentment melted and turned into excitement at the prospect of having a real child in the house.

Yet, when he arrived home early, he questioned the reality:

'How do you *know*?'

'Because I just *do*.'

'But how? Explain it to me.'

'I can't.'

'Just try.'

'I tried. You didn't listen.'

'Try again.'

And so on, into the night, until they were exhausted and merely collapsed in one another's arms, only because they had no energy to do otherwise.

In the morning, over tea and scones, Caitlin talked with excitement about her plans: the decorator, the new furniture; the clothes shopping; the first birthday party; the blanket she would knit.

'But we don't even know if it's a boy or a girl yet,' protested Paul.

'We don't need to. I'll get pink and blue of everything,' returned Caitlin.

And so it went, all week, with the launching of shopping expeditions, the drafting of decorating plans, the booking of doctor appointments, the interviewing of babysitters, and the reading of books on birthing. It was a whirlwind of excitement and hopefulness – building for the future. It occurred to Caitlin as she asked for the sales clerk to bring her the rattan chair in both pink and blue cushions that she had never had to plan anything so complex before. Her wedding her mother had taken charge of, from the invitations the whole way through to the honeymoon, all carefully orchestrated to be perfect – at least for the parents. But this was her own. It didn't appear to her as a symbol of maturity but instead as magic that she had prayed for – not a natural progression but something progressively unnatural.

One day, tired after a long day shopping, Caitlin sat on a wooden bench in the centre of the quaint Westbridge shopping district. After some time a small girl, not older than eight, sat next to her.

'I'm waiting for my mommy,' she explained as she crossed her leotarded legs on the bench.

Caitlin looked at the girl. 'Did you know that I'm a mommy too?'

'You don't look like a mommy,' replied the girl quickly, with consummate assurance and a critical eye.

'But I am.'

'Then where's your child?'

'Right here.' Caitlin draped her palm over the still flat plane of her stomach.

'There's no room in there for a child,' replied the girl mightily.

'Listen.' Caitlin beckoned the girl to place an ear against her.

The girl complied to hear the murmurings of life. 'Nothing's there,' she pronounced after a dutiful moment.

'Oh no. Listen carefully.'

But then along came her mother and the girl scampered away.

When the pregnancy test result finally arrived, it was as unnecessary as it was positive. Caitlin was already long

MISBEGOTTEN

used to being a mother. She imagined the sensitivity of the soul inside her, conceived as it was in the name of poetry. It was odd not to know the father except from a few lines on a questionnaire. At different points in the day, she took to imagining him – his physique, his bearing. She was surprised that it interested her as much as it did. After all, Dotterweich had explained that Paul would be the father, and he would be. But what then was this other being? Just a dollop of sperm on a spoon? Or a donor, doleful at his shadowy role? A father too, with feelings and longings? It didn't take Caitlin long to start dreaming up scenarios for his current state. He was clearly a higher being, consumed with the love and creation of poetry. But did children interest him? Perhaps not, except as abstractions. Or was he a poet with a huge family already, so fertile that his fertility could only run over into a stranger's cup? Sometimes, she imagined him a tragic genius, unable to relate to the world – donating his sperm so that he could at least have poetic progeny, wired to convey his artistic currency to the next generation.

At times, all these imaginings haunted her. To imagine something that's truly in the land of make-believe is an indulgence without consequence. But to imagine something that in fact resides within you, that has lodged itself as thoroughly in your innards as an organ itself, can be frightening; the consequences are all too compelling. Like the horror of illness, it cannot be walked away from. Wherever you go, so goes the breast cancer or the enlarged prostate or the epileptic seizures. With any other type of problem, there's somewhere to hide: you can jump into the brambles of chapter eleven to evade bankruptcy; or move to the West Coast to run clear from your relatives on the East; or rush into the arms of another man to forget the one that hurt you. But where do you go to forsake your lymphoma? If not into the realm of prayer, then where?

To Caitlin, pregnancy was ominously similar. Despite the joys she felt at the initial conception, she was sometimes plagued by feelings she didn't dare give voice to: that the child she was carrying was not really hers but someone else's – a someone else she didn't know, a stranger. Perhaps a monster. There was no avoiding the two new people within her: her child and her child's precursor. In the time of a second, Caitlin could go from calm to frenzy at the prospect. A coagulating doubt hardened around her by night. Only to thin with the brightness of day.

But the uncertainty of the being within her was as complex as her personality was wont to make it. She couldn't help but be at the mercy of the full force of her impulsive imagination. The pain of loosening the imaginative screws lay in the corresponding tightening of those which imprisoned her.

An incident that occurred a day before the artificial insemination worried her especially. She went to sleep early, in preparation for the clinic visit. She was half asleep when an hour later Paul slid under the covers. She felt his hand unaccustomedly groping her thighs. In his hard touch there was something desperate and hurtful. She tried to roll over and sleep, but he slithered on top of her and lifted her nightgown, breathing quickly and wheezily. Soon he was inside her.

'What are you doing?' she imagined asking him.

'I'm sure as hell going to fuck you before the test tube does,' he replied in her imagination.

But she endured the dry and silent lovemaking until he

rolled off her. Then, sore and tired, she concentrated on falling asleep.

In Dotterweich's office three days later, forty-eight hours after being inseminated, Caitlin mentioned still being sore.

'The procedure may have caused it. It will disappear shortly. Not to fear,' he replied.

'It wasn't from the procedure.'

'Oh?'

'It was from sex the night before the insemination. Paul wanted it.'

Dotterweich laughed. 'I see. That's not uncommon. Many couples wish to meld their own sexual act to the artificial conception – at least in their psyches. That way they can feel responsible. Especially husbands. It's to be expected. It's perhaps healthy psychologically.' Dotterweich fisted his small hands and shook them mightily. 'The power of the evolutionary surge is always there. It's best to give in to it. This way Paul will be more comfortable with your child. He can mentally claim it as his own.' He relaxed his posture and crossed his arms on his chest. 'A father, as I've told you, is a reproductive entity, trying desperately, often savagely, to scatter his seed into the next generation. That Paul was severely threatened by a biochemical substitute, a creature of technology, a test tube if you will, is understandable. His sexual act was a reclamation of his biological purpose. In his mind, he can now pretend he's the father. In fact, with his timing he could be the father.'

Caitlin was only half listening, quite accustomed to Dotterweich's lecturing style, thinking too of the glorious birth that awaited her, joyously considering the happiness she would feel when she indeed was informed she was pregnant. But at Dotterweich's last words, she pricked up her ears.

'What did you say?'

Dotterweich laughed again. 'I said it's funny because with his timing, I mean the night before, the child could end up being his after all.'

Caitlin blanched. 'How so? If he's infertile?'

'Of course. But he's not *completely* infertile. I mean his percentages – his viable sperm counts – are low. And he's never yet impregnated you. But that doesn't mean he hasn't a healthy sperm there somewhere. He could *possibly* impregnate you. Not likely. But if you asked me, could he? I would have to say it's possible.'

Caitlin felt a strange and unpleasant tingling at this news. 'But how would we ever know just who is the father?'

'Well, we could run paternity tests. But I think that you'll know.' Dotterweich winked. 'Mothers always know. It's another evolutionary instinct. The most primeval of instincts. Being aware of your protector. You'll know. And then, perhaps, you will be very lucky and the child will turn out to be Paul's.'

Upon seeing Caitlin's wan face, Dotterweich realised he shouldn't have mentioned it to her. It was a strict policy of his never to discuss this possibility with patients, lest they begin to think they should have persisted in trying naturally, though it could have taken years and then still been fruitless.

Though she said nothing further and quickly left the office, Caitlin was mulling over this news. The thought that her child could now, after all that emotionalism, be Paul's, upset her. Not because they'd spent all this money and time hunting for a donor. And not because she felt that Dotterweich had been more than deceitful in the way he'd safeguarded this information until now. But because she did not want this baby to be Paul's.

For her, now, the child was a fantasy. A fantasy of another life worth living. With another man in imagination if not in reality. A genetic imprint from outside anything she knew which simultaneously scared, thrilled and inspired her. She couldn't return to a prosaic interpretation: a baby so like many others; a child sired by Paul. He wasn't worthy. His genes weren't worth passing on.

On the way home, she drove erratically and zipped through an intersection, ignoring a stop sign and nearly getting tagged by a Mercedes. *No, it wouldn't be Paul's*, she thought finally. As Dotterweich had said, mothers always know. And she convinced herself, emphatically – as though it couldn't be otherwise – that this baby would not be Paul's. Yet as she drove up the gravel drive, struggling to feel the imperceptible rumblings of the new beginnings inside her, she had to admit she wasn't quite sure.

18

He took the small slip of paper, now graced with his neat, florid script, and with a grin as succinct as his verse, read:

For poetry's sake –
Not for money, or love, or any part of flesh.
Will your child find its worldly way.

He sealed the page in a stamped envelope and left it on the desk.

Then he got in the cab and enjoyed the tired purr of the engine and the languid sound of the muzak on the radio. It took no time to reach the clinic – traffic was light after midnight – and soon he was standing in front of the clear glass doors with his burglary tools.

He was still grinning: grinning at the ease of everything, the aplomb with which he could stand here and contemplate this crime – this crime, more horrible than any other – whereby he would steal a woman's mind, identity and hopes. At this, the last moment of her anonymity, he found the familiar gnawing reach his heart and signal his excitement. Within minutes he would know her name and her address. Within minutes he would put a face on this amorphous desperation that he knew was there lurking somewhere in one of those suburban homes, hoping for a child.

He jemmied the lock easily and walked to the alarm keypad where he entered the security code as if he had done it a thousand times before. Crapshoot did it as authoritatively as the secretary had earlier that morning when he, with high-powered binoculars trained carefully, had sat in the cab and memorised the numbers she punched. Then he found his way to Dotterweich's office and jemmied that lock as well. The file cabinets sat there waiting. He marvelled at the real lack of security afforded such a collection of destinies. There were no video cameras, no motion detectors. Just locks and alarms. And locks and alarms would stop no one, certainly not him. Only locks and alarms between him and someone else's much-needed privacy – between him and the face on all that desperation.

Later, at the taxi stand, with excitement welling up inside him and threatening to overflow, he returned to the envelope where he'd left it. It looked sadly barren without an address and he sat down to remedy that. He copied it from recent memory on to the envelope, slowly despite his enthusiasm, with relish, imagining the future mother opening it:

Mrs Caitlin Bourke
15 Stepping Hill Road
Westbridge, Connecticut
05455

There. The timing would be perfect. And what an elegant envelope he'd selected for this task, the type he used for all important business transactions. The best of papers for the best of intentions.

Crapshoot's hand drifted down to the linen of his crotch and felt a warm stickiness seeping through the fabric. A little of this he then rubbed on the envelope right below the address. *Yes, the best of papers for the best of intentions.*

19

Only a skilful stripper could compete with the daily mail call for its flirtatious promise and corresponding disappointment. Every day Caitlin waited for the chance to go out to the shiny black box at the end of the driveway and fetch the new mail. She always felt a slightly dulled excitement on that short walk, almost sexual, that heightened at the moment she pulled down the flap of the door and saw the stack of envelopes. As she got back to the house, she registered the parade of the painfully unmagical: bills, solicitations, postcards from acquaintances, pre-approved credit applications. What she was hoping for in that morning mail forever eluded her, both in mind and under the postmark. She knew not – even in her imagination – what it could be. Many people hope to find the winning sweepstakes entry but in that Caitlin wasn't interested; she had never lacked for money. She couldn't delude herself that riches would solve everything. Sometimes she thought her wish was for a letter from a caring friend that would set the day right. But then, there in the folds of that letter, she found very little that could transform reality: a few anecdotes that would make her laugh, gossip, some genuine emotion that only heightened poignantly the silence of her many rooms.

Once, there had been a letter from an old lover. Upon seeing the return address, she was intrigued. Expectant, she had delicately sliced through the top of it with her sharp silver letter opener. Then she pulled out two glossy pieces – the halves of an enclosed photo, severed by her own hand – a familiar man (still handsome in a tux) in one, and his pretty bride in the other. The accompanying note apologised for not inviting her to the wedding and assumed she understood. She did.

That same day a Federal Express package arrived. Usually such things were for her husband, but this one was addressed to her. She opened it quickly. Inside, much to her disappointment, was the American Express card replacement she'd ordered.

That afternoon she took the card shopping. She spent over $3000. After all, there was no pre-set limit to either her expenditure or her despair.

So today as usual, at mail call, she expected, for no good reason, something out of the ordinary. If it was only bills and supermarket circulars, she would have been, as she always was, surprised.

But today was different, she told herself as she walked along the gravel.

She reached into the box and pulled out only one piece of mail. The envelope paper was delicate – onion skin – of a type she hadn't seen in years. Though there was no return address, her name was neatly penned. A single sheet was contained in the envelope and she spread it slowly on the kitchen table. There were few words and what words there were perplexed her. She read them over and over again:

For poetry's sake –
Not for money, or love, or any part of flesh.
Will your child find its worldly way.

MISBEGOTTEN

It appeared to be a short poem, like a haiku, of the type she used to scribble hastily in the inside covers of her binder when bored during her classes in college. It didn't hit her until she had walked all the way back up the drive that these words had not found their way mistakenly into her mailbox.

For poetry's sake.

She clutched her belly and winced. Dotterweich was the first thought that occurred to her. *That sick, fat prick.* Was this his idea of a practical joke? Or just more scientific experimentation?

She ran to the phone in the kitchen.

'Yes, give me Dr Dotterweich, please. This is Caitlin Bourke.'

A short pause.

'Hello Mrs Bourke, Dotterweich here. How are you feeling?'

'Did you send this note?'

Another pause.

'What note?'

'This poem.'

'Of course not.'

'Then *he* did.'

'What poem, Mrs Bourke?'

'I'll read it to you. Just a second. Here: *For poetry's sake – not for money or love or any part of flesh will your child find its worldly way.*'

'Mrs Bourke, sit down.'

'I'm not sitting. Tell me what's this about.'

'Mrs Bourke, you're under a significant amount of stress. Now you don't want to upset your pregnancy by getting agitated. Please sit down and try to relax.'

'I am relaxed.'

'Mrs Bourke, is Paul home?'

'Of course not. He's never home.'

'Mrs Bourke. We all have inevitable difficulties adjusting to the psychological rigours of pregnancy. You will find that fantasies about the donor are quite natural – even expected. To fantasise about such communications, even to long for them ... There is a process of transference, of a biological connection trying to assert itself through the realm of man's interventions. It's perfectly natural. But try not to get carried away by it. Give in to it somewhat – indulge it just a jot, perhaps – but don't cross the line. It could be damaging, dangerous.'

'What are you talking about?'

'I'm talking about what's a very emotional time for you – the realisation that you are carrying another man's genetic imprint, another man's life and dreams. But make them your own, Mrs Bourke, for they are your own at this point. It is *normal* to feel this – '

'I'm not making this up. I don't know what you're talking about. I got this poem in the mail today, addressed to me. I'll fax it to you so you can see – '

'Mrs Bourke. Please. There's no need to fax anything. Please. Take a deep breath – '

'It's a written note – a poem – addressed to me. I'm not imagining it. I'm holding it right here in my hand, OK? Jesus – '

'Mrs Bourke. Please. Calm. Take a deep breath.'

Pause.

'Good. Now, Mrs Bourke, what, may I ask, is the return address on this poem?'

'There's none. That's the – '

'OK. Now please, Mrs Bourke, I know how difficult this all is for you. I – '

MISBEGOTTEN

Caitlin slammed the phone into the cradle and ran out of the house, down the drive, and out to the road to look for the mail truck. There was nothing. A fog had set in and there were no cars. Only the swaying of the tree branches overhead and a slight whistling as the wind took hold.

Back in the bedroom, Caitlin sat on the plush carpeting and spread out the poem on her lap. She smelled the paper, held it to the light, examined the scrawl closely – all to cull from those crude measures the identity of the sender.

Her donor had written to her. That much was clear. But how? Why?

There was dignity in those lines. It was a poem – and a beautiful one at that, she decided. She stood and went to her night table and found a copy of the donor's application. She reread the line: *For poetry's sake.* Yes, *he* had written to her. And about time it was, really. Dotterweich certainly didn't understand. She had been curious. And when she thought about it, she had been waiting. And *he* had read her mind. Yes, she had been waiting. There was no doubt about that. All of a sudden, the logic was undeniable.

She began to imagine *his* identity, personality, features. But then she didn't dare.

With time.

There were nearly nine months to get to know each other. Nine long months.

20

He recalled trying on his mother's pumps and négligé as a child and feeling immediately a girl. Such a sudden transformation alarmed him at first. But in it was power. And over time Crapshoot grew grateful for the chameleon-like methods and talents that allowed him to be whoever or whatever he wanted to be, whenever or for whatever reason he wanted to be it.

Of late he was a poet.

And just the mere affectation of certain things had made it so: a new tilt to the head, a new lilt to the thoughts; a pen in pocket, a pad in hand. The props were simple, really. As cons went, it was low overhead. Being a poet meant observing. Pausing to see what he'd never seen. He fashioned himself into an artist. But mostly an *artiste*. And he knew instinctively that the secret of all artistry is to be alone. Solitude he was no stranger to. And so he was predisposed. For the biggest challenge to the beginner was feeling a purpose to one's days when the only purpose that presents itself is the empty page. But what really inspired, delighted, spurred and tantalised him was the promise of some cold, hard cash.

Crapshoot now spent most mornings at the taxi stand drafting. It had become easier and easier to construct a poem. With a dictionary at one elbow and a thesaurus at the other, he was well equipped. Today he was working on a masterpiece and paused only now and then to take a sip from his coffee. The coffee tasted bitter anyway – as bitter as his melancholy. And the images he chose to spin into verse were absolutely depressing. Here and again he would choose to spot some new attack, a new adventure for his mind's meanderings. What really delighted his senses, however, was the promise that these poems foretold: the promise of a soul to be hooked, trapped, exploited and harassed – and owned.

For within each image, each verse, each couplet and each rhyme lay a vision of his target: a lonely woman, embarking on childhood, with his genetic imprint – the legacy of his semen. That he was so much in control of this destiny excited him. He knew so much about her fate – but she, so little of his. The code of his biology had insinuated itself into her loins. But her touch, her perfume, her lips, were still foreign to him. But, of course, seduction moves slowly – and seduction through poetry moves the slowest of all. It's careful, mellifluous and indirect. But when it hits, it hits hard. And such hardness he was counting on.

He lifted his pen and scrawled another verse:

You and I
Poetry in motion
A biological link.
Our identities mere whispers
Only after dark.

Though pleased with the lack of effort it had taken him to create those words, he worried about their effect. Would she appreciate them? Would she cry? Would she realise the import of his designs? Would she be scared, touched, hurt, delighted? He wished for an amalgam of those emotions. Something heretofore unfelt. Indescribable.

He knew that the best confidence games are the result of misdirection. A shell game is a shell game. And poetry was just another shell game.

As a three card monte dealer, he'd learned the importance of ambiguity. In the games he used to run, in Central Park, in the Mall, in spring, by early evening – when the suckers came out – the hand was always his. How? Easy. It would be a pleasant sixty degrees, sweater weather by nightfall. And pedestrians would funnel through the Mall, past the Halfshell, and over to his booth, on the way out of the park. A father or a mother, a child or a teen. Each one in turn would come over to his table and bet a hand. First they would watch, seduced by the intimacy of the table, the cards flying in all directions.

Everyone knows the rules of three card monte. There lies the secret. Because an intimate knowledge of the rules goads you into a false confidence. And when the rules are so simple, by definition, the *game* never can be. You hold two black kings – spades and clubs – and one red queen, and the idea is to shuttle your cards lightning fast, and mislead the viewer. So that he or she can never tell where the queen finally falls. When it does fall, you challenge the viewer to point to it. But the viewer never can. What once was red is now black. What once was black is blood red. The trickery is all in the misdirection.

There is only one rule, Crapshoot used to say, to three card monte: *make the sucker feel special*. In that was the key to the game. And to most games. Or, at least, con games.

On a slow day, towards nightfall, when everyone else had left, a young boy approached the table – two cardboard boxes stacked one atop the other – and asked if he could play. Crapshoot adjusted his carnation and smiled.

'Card games are for grownups, young tadpole. Don't you know that?'

'I'm good at card games. Good as any grownup.'

'Well, we'll see,' replied Crapshoot, spinning the cards fast as can be, round and round, in a manic shuffle. Then purposefully slowing, showing a little red here and there, drawing the boy's eyes down and then abruptly waving his hand over the silent cards. 'Where's the red queen?'

The boy, dressed in a turtleneck with blue stripes across the belly and a thin thatch of brown hair, pointed confidently to the middle card.

Crapshoot hiked up one side of his mouth in mock surprise and flipped the card over with his thumbnail. 'I'll be, young tadpole. That's a red queen you spied with your eagle eye. But that's because no money's riding on it. You'd crack with the pressure of a real hand.'

To answer his challenge the young boy reached into his pocket and withdrew a crumpled bill. 'Five dollars, this time.'

Crapshoot looked at him disapprovingly. 'Didn't your mother ever tell you not to gamble? Now put that money away.'

'My mom's dead,' the boy replied simply, casually.

'Well then your father must have told you something about gambling...'

'Daddy lives out West. I live with my grandma.'

'And where is your grandmother right now?'

'She's at home, watching TV, in Bwooklyn,' he swallowed the R.

'A young tadpole, as froglike as you are, should not be gambling. Now scram.'

'I'm going to win.'

'If you're so sure, let's try it one more time with no money at all, OK? Let's see if you have *that special touch*.'

'A'right.'

Crapshoot shuffled the cards again, this time flipping, gnashing and buckling them – imposing trick upon trick – then giving him another gift by showing a glimmer of red right before the landing. 'Well?'

The boy picked the queen again. 'There. Easy.'

'You are good, young man. But I don't take five-dollar bets anyway. So beat it.'

The boy reached into his pocket again and pulled out another bill. 'Here's a twenty.'

Crapshoot looked at the crumpled bill. 'What's your name, young hustler?'

'Kyle.'

Crapshoot patted him gently on the shoulder. 'I'm Billy. Nice to meet you, Kyle. I'll tell you what. I'll let you bet your twenty-five dollars. *But*: if you lose, you have to promise to act like a grownup and not cry.' Crapshoot looked at the boy sternly. 'Promise?'

'I promise.' It was the promise of one who doesn't take the vow seriously, seeing no need to.

'You have to swear on your mother's grave.'

The boy looked down. 'I swear on my mother's grave.'

'Fine. Now, place your twenty-five dollars right there next to the cards, like a grownup. Good. Now watch the cards. Watch the red queen.'

'OK.'

Crapshoot started slow, showing red every now and then, then sped up to a vicious fury, and slowed back down again, showing the last bit of red and, just as quickly, invisibly shuttling it over to the left, where it didn't belong.

'So?'

The boy pointed at the far card. 'There.'

'You have to put your money where your mouth is, Kyle. Winter ball is over. This is the big leagues. Put your bills on the card.'

'OK.'

The boy smoothed out the twenty and the five and stacked them on top. Crapshoot flipped the card over and just as quickly slipped the bills into his pants pocket. The king of clubs lay face up on the box.

'Kyle, I told you to watch carefully. Those red queens fly like banshees.'

A tear, ever so slightly, started to form in the corner of the young boy's eye. Crapshoot watched it grow and grow.

'Remember your vows, tadpole,' said Crapshoot, snapping up the money and cards, kicking the cardboard table away and walking off into the night.

Crapshoot sealed the verse in an envelope. His cab started smoothly. Spring had come and though there were no flowers here in Northport, there was finally the warmth of the fledgling sun. The back roads to Westbridge were still wet with the short rain of the morning and Crapshoot took the turns carefully. After twenty minutes' driving, he came to a stop light. A large red Mercedes with a well-preserved older blonde at the wheel pulled alongside him, signalling the entrance into Westbridge country. It tempted him a bit. He shrugged it off: merely an omen of far greater plans.

He used the stop light as an opportunity to remove his camera from the glove compartment and check the settings. Then he got his bearings and mentally recalled the route. He smiled. His memory was excellent. As it should

MISBEGOTTEN

be. After three such prior trips, he had no excuse not to know these Westbridge roads well: a turn on to Stepping Ridge Road, then a left on to the majestic, oak-lined Yeoman's Way, bear left at the fork, a half a mile down into the gulch-like hollow. The mailbox sat pleasantly perched – a bird in wait for the daily feast, and for the sometime disgorging. Crapshoot looked around at the trees and the silence. He rolled down his window and opened the box carefully. There were four letters: three pieces of junk mail and one note addressed on personal stationery. Crapshoot took the note. It was meticulously addressed, in fine, neatly rounded penmanship, to 15 Stepping Hill Road, Westbridge, CT. From his glove compartment, he retrieved another letter – one similarly addressed by the same hand, which he had borrowed a week earlier and had since read, photocopied, and meticulously resealed – and placed it in the box with his other letter.

Then Crapshoot closed the mailbox, backed the car up fifty yards, pulled to the side and got out. On foot, camera in hand, he walked into the woods – careful not to soil his suit on the wet brambles – and headed in the direction of the house.

When he was well positioned, on a small hillock that provided a good view, down and away past the trees and into the angles of the sprawling house, he knelt. He used the telephoto lens to observe particulars of the house's construction and duly noted them in his head, before snapping a photo of each one. Then photographed the Range Rover in the driveway, the empty deck, the front door. The patio in the rear, off the kitchen, where the security lights didn't reach.

It was the sort of house he wouldn't necessarily mind

living in. He did a quick analysis of the acreage, the setting, the house's condition, expanse, square footage and exposures, and assessed the value at just over a million.

It was a large white Dutch colonial with newer additions on either side. The eaves and front door were detailed in forest green. A gravel circular driveway surrounded a symmetrical planting of conifer shrubs. A sundial sat embedded in the centre, silently recording the shadows. *She* was home – *somewhere*.

That was enough for today, thought Crapshoot, heading back to his taxicab. On the way, he glanced at the mailbox and considered his poem inside: a red queen it was now. But what would it be by the time she, so trusting, reached for it?

21

'Gin!' called out Serena, folding her cards on to the table. 'Three queens and a run of hearts.'

'That's your match,' said Caitlin, feigning disappointment. She added her cards to Serena's. 'I shouldn't have shuffled that time. I'm bad luck for myself.'

'Aren't we all?' said Serena, raising her eyebrows. 'I mean that's what it's all about. I've been bad luck for myself for as long as I can remember. And after two glasses of wine, honey, I'm the worst luck you've ever seen.'

That was true, thought Caitlin. But it hardly took half a glass. 'Where's Kent going tonight?'

'Out,' said Serena, rolling her eyes. She crossed her legs and looked down. 'I don't know. Out – drinking with the boys . . . or the girls. I could hardly give a shit, really.'

Caitlin looked away. Paul was out too, away in Tucson on business. 'Another glass?'

Serena held her empty crystal to the light. 'Would you?' Caitlin poured. 'What about you, girl?'

'You know I can't.'

'Oh, right, of course. The *baby*. Listen, sweetness, I drank my little ones into a stupor every night they sat in my womb and they turned out to have two arms and two legs. You can't let those doctors brainwash you. You *have* to continue to have *fun.*' Serena leaned forward and put her hand on Caitlin's knee.

The *baby*.

Serena uttered that word with such a lack of maternity that Caitlin placed her own hand on her belly in a compensating impulse.

The silhouettes of the coming dusk projected through the sunlights, along the eggshell-white wall paint, off the bottle of Pouilly-Fuissé, and on to the mahogany coffee table.

'So who's the daddy, anyway?' asked Serena, reclining along the long white couch.

'Who's the daddy?' replied Caitlin to stall for time, uncertain of how much she wanted to disclose.

'Yes, *whom* did you fuck?' asked Serena with wide eyes and a toothy smile. 'Or shall I say, who knocked you up, darling? The test tube did it, right? But come on ... Don't be ashamed. I won't tell anyone.'

Caitlin considered her predicament. How strange to be even asked such a question. *Who was the father of her child?* The slight movements she detected in her belly would seem to foretell the answer somehow – until she would lean forward and the sensation would fade. Nausea on a regular basis seemed to foretell the answer too. But it merely posed the question. The tension of something growing inside her yielded to the flexibility of her imagination.

The promise of the child was more real than anything she'd ever felt before. Yet, there was something unreal – something terrifying, too. The mystery of pregnancy is such that it robs you of your self-indulgence. All of a sudden, bodily urges and functions exist for two people: for two the heart beats, the lungs expand, the vessels dilate, the stomach digests, the appetite craves. No longer does a body satisfy itself. There's a responsibility for another. And with such responsibility comes fear.

Caitlin had never cared for anyone but herself. But now her body gave her no option. Her destiny was interlinked with another. And seemingly, of late, with yet a third. She remembered the cool, clinical nature of the procedure and Dr Dotterweich's stares of supervision. But it never occurred to her that at that moment – the very moment that the sperm were shunted into her uterus, like so many commuting Buicks into the Lincoln Tunnel – a third someone, the biological father, would be sitting in the wings, poised for a dramatic entry. Romance through the mail. And through her womb.

But Serena was not the person to confide in. Caitlin felt that instinctively. There was something about Serena's own experience with childbearing that stood in the way. And there was something about a best friend that was never really understanding – the same way a car alarm was never really alarming; the way a reunion never really reunited anyone.

'I have no idea.'

Serena clapped. 'You have no idea?!'

'That's right.'

'Well, how's that – to have no idea, I mean. Lord, it's like you were raped or something. Just like some guy in a bar ripped off your panties and your brassière and then let you have it. That's some naughty stuff, Caitlin. You should write it down in your diary or something.'

'It's not like that.'

Serena clapped again. 'Whatever it's like ... doesn't matter.' She lowered her voice. 'How 'bout something completely outrageous?'

Caitlin grimaced.

'Oh please!' Serena finished the wine, head tossed back. 'Please don't turn mommy on me – at least not yet. You *cannot* say no. I won't let you.'

'What have you got in mind, Serena?' Caitlin considered the possibilities. Last year it had been cocaine on the cold leather of a limo careening down the West Side Highway. The year before that it was Christmas carolling in fur coats and nothing else with too much eggnog and not enough shame. Once, it had been picking up college boys at a local bar. And then there was bribing the cops after doing three wine coolers and more than eighty miles per hour on the Westbridge back roads.

'This.' Serena handed over a worn piece of newspaper.

'*Hard body. GQ looks. Buns of steel. Ladies only. Expensive. 25 minute response time. Service all Fairfield County. 864–2122*,' read Caitlin limply.

'Sounds tremendous, no?'

'Sounds like a gigolo.'

'Should I call or should you?'

'Why don't you call, Serena. I'm going to bed.'

Serena grabbed her arm. 'What did I tell you? You're not a mommy yet. Have a little fun. We'll see if he's up to the challenge of two Westbridge babes.' Serena's eyes were glazed with the wine and the image of it. 'Or we'll just make him dance for us. A dancing slave with buns of steel. That's safe, right? I'll crank up the Madonna and we'll make this hunk perform. How'd you like to see the look on Paul's face when he comes in and sees that going on, huh? Paul Bourke standing in his Brooks Brothers khakis in that corner ... and *GQ* Buns-of-Steel in a G-string in that corner. What do you say, Caitlin?'

'I said, *you* call. *I'm* going to bed.'

*

MISBEGOTTEN

Before sliding under the covers that night, Caitlin took out the small paper she had hidden inside her pillowcase and reread the lines she'd already glossed so many times:

You and I
Poetry in motion
A biological link.
Our identities mere whispers
Only after dark.

Those whispers were a part of her now as she tumbled blissfully under the goosedown comforter and relished the darkness of her room and the lonely monocle of light of the lamp that illumined her reading. Without Paul, the space seemed so open, the bed vast, the sheets cool and inviting, yet profoundly deserted. She reread the lines again and again, feeling their resonance as they tumbled along, their meaning unfettered, unadulterated – absolutely potent. She'd never known that words could so affect her. Only five lines. But five lines that celebrated the biological transformations that nourished her belly – five lines that were the very source of it. Soon, the paper still clutched in hand and the light still pulling shadows from the nether corners of her bed, she slept.

In the morning Caitlin came down groggy to the smell of a fresh pot of coffee percolating. Serena was at the stove, tending lazily to a few pieces of French toast. A young handsome man, not more than twenty, was sitting at the table, his dark locks happily dishevelled, his buff musculature well defined, even through Paul's terrycloth bathrobe. He smiled absurdly.

'Caitlin, this is Troy, Troy meet Caitlin. This is her

house,' said Serena, the smoky residue of last night still attached to every word.

Caitlin nodded and sat down to burnt French toast with Serena and Troy. One happy family.

22

He showed them the photos: breasts, lingerie, Technicolor lips.

'She's eighteen. Barely legal. And this one ... she's a dancer, she's perfect with the other. They love each other. And they'll love you ...'

'How much?' asked the bald one.

Crapshoot frowned. He hated rude questions. This was a rude question. He adjusted his carnation and tie. Being well dressed was essential to this particular game.

'You have perhaps heard the phrase *the time of your life*? This will be that classic time. For both you chaps.' Crapshoot smiled magnanimously across the seat of the Cadillac. It was dark and headlights periodically frosted the rearview. He would have to stall them a bit.

His thoughts drifted to his more important quarry: where was *she* right now? What were her thoughts? And did they revolve around him? Had she received his letters? To imagine any answer to these questions excited his curiosity further. The very questioning titillated him and he felt the gnawing – cruder now in its growing lust. He turned his attention back to the less interesting lust before him.

The other man spoke. He had a mouth that moved in a

perpetual yawn, with its oval slowness and shape. 'He asked how much.'

Crapshoot winked. 'A thousand.'

'For the night?'

It was important to drive the bargain hard, and then concede something. *Make the sucker feel special.* Crapshoot smiled inwardly at the circularity of all things. The basic rules always applied. That was the magic of it. And on a night like tonight, when the cops ruled the streets and gunshots were too dangerous, you had to be creative.

'For one hour. The two of them.'

The bald one laughed and tossed the photos on to the seat. 'Get out.' But it was the yawner who stayed in the game. 'How about five hundred?'

'A thousand for the two. It's not worth it to them to take less than that. But I'll make it two hours.'

The bald one craned his neck to exchange a glance with the yawner. He nodded. 'A'right. A grand for the two for two hours. Now where?'

Crapshoot picked the photos from the floor. He spoke slowly: 'The beauty of Star is that she's absolutely outgoing and eager to please. Her sole purpose is to cater to your needs,' he said wistfully, holding the photo up for the yawner's benefit. The yawner was the gameplayer. The consummate sucker. The show now had to be directed to him. 'The beauty of Amber is that she's a Scorpio and you know what eighteen-year-old Scorpios are like – insatiable and sensual, kind and generous. She was born so recently. Perhaps you could teach her a few things – '

'Where?'

'At the Nightcap Inn. I have them in a room there. It's clean, beverages on hand. If you want to really party, I have coke for a small extra fee. All the amenities. Perfect.

MISBEGOTTEN

They're both there right now, in their lingerie, waiting for you – '

'Let's go.'

'But ... I need to know you're serious. Show me the bills.'

'We'll get them to you at the hotel.'

'Fine.'

Ten minutes later, they pulled into the motel parking lot. Now was the beautiful moment – when he had to crank up the pace like the rhythm of a samba. He had to make these boys nervous – give them sweaty palms. With sweaty palms, they would have to conclude this deal. Sweaty palms would make the bills wilt away from their wallets with ease. Crapshoot loved this part. This was the ultimate test of his unscrupulous abilities. From nothing to create something.

He would do the same with Caitlin: create something between them where no bond had hitherto existed. It was alchemy, plain and simple. The sperm helped, of course. To be the father was to be a part of her life. Maybe it was cheap, but he loved it all the same. He knew that she would feel special very soon – like any sucker. But she would be his *for ever*.

'Now. For an extra twenty I'll watch the car until you're done. You never know in this neighbourhood. And another thing: undercover cops keep a weather eye out in this lot, mostly for drug deals, so move quickly. Don't dawdle. Take the elevators in the back of the lobby. Have you got that?' He turned to the yawner, who looked nervous in the eyes. *Perfect.* 'Now you give me the bills and I give you the room number.' The bald one looked hesitant. 'Hurry up. Five minutes sitting still in this lot is the wrong thing to do – gets the wrong kind of attention.'

Crapshoot pointed to a Ford LTD sitting in the parking lot. 'That there's an undercover police cruiser. Don't worry: they're looking for drugs, but ... OK. Now the bills ...'

The bald one pulled out hundreds from his billfold and counted them, hands shaking slightly. Ten.

Crapshoot folded the bills slowly, recounting them like a blackjack dealer at the five-dollar table. Nine.

'You missed one, slick.'

The bald one was nervous now. He reached in for another bill. 'There you go. What's the fucking room number?'

'Three-fourteen. You got that. Third floor, off the elevators, take a left, knock once – then twice – you got that?' They nodded. 'And twenty more to have me watch the car. Remember?'

'Don't got a twenty.'

'Well ...'

The bald one pulled out yet another hundred. 'Watch it good,' he said, more to soothe his pride that he'd clinched a decent deal than out of real concern.

'Right. Now, call them by their names – Star, Amber – when they come to the door. Remember that. If you forget the names, they won't open the door. Got it?'

'Got it.' The bald one started to leave.

'And another thing. A hundred for the hotel security. You gentlemen don't want to get busted, do you?'

Yet another bill changed hands. 'Good. Now rest assured – you will enjoy. If you don't see me parked in front when you get out, then walk around to the Francis Street side. I'll be waiting in the shadows near the dumpster.'

They got out of the Cadillac and walked towards the lobby doors. Then the bald one turned to come back.

MISBEGOTTEN

Damn, what now?

The bald one leaned into the window and smiled, 'How do we know these girls'll be the ones in the photos?' *Good*, that was a worry he could handle.

'If they're not, come back down.'

'And?'

'And, I give you your money back.'

'And ... if you've taken off with the cash and the car? What then?'

The *big* question. They were not nervous enough, that was clear. He would call their bluff.

'All right. Park the car yourself. I'll come upstairs with you.'

The bald one smiled. He looked assured. 'Forget it. See you in a couple hours. Just remember: if you're not here, I'm coming after you.'

Crapshoot merely smiled back, graciously. 'Have the time of your life.'

The bald one joined the yawner at the bank of elevators in the lobby and pressed the button. Crapshoot watched them enter the elevator and head towards nothing. Then he rolled slowly out of the parking lot and checked his watch.

On the way back to downtown Northport, he looked for the garage signal. He sorted his optical nerves into three batches: one for the signal, another for the rearview, and the third for the road ahead. His mind wandered to the glorious con-cum-striptease that he had performed. He'd been somewhat worried when the bald one made a bit of trouble. But the essential property of any con was its malleability – the way it twisted and turned to mould itself to the particular dupe's type of trust.

Even better was when it adapted to a lack of trust, like a comedian adapting to a lack of laughter in the crowd and turning it to his advantage. A true pro always knew how to mock that silence, to twist it and make that very unfunniness funny. And there was nothing better in the world of cons, thought Crapshoot, than to be challenged so utterly by a cynical soul. With a cynical soul you had to work extra hard to convey that glorious special attention which so often resulted in the kill. Just as a comedian with a slow crowd had to work all the harder to get a laugh.

There was the signal: a bonfire in a garbage can at Tannery Square. So they were under the bridge tonight. He drove methodically, right, left, the underpass – into the garage. He dropped off the car for the new paint and the new plates. Then he collected the money.

Ten minutes later he sat in the darkened taxi stand. He pushed away the shallow cauldron of ashes that sat cool after the day's work. He had told them so many times not to smoke near his desk.

Pulling out a piece of elegant paper from the drawer, he mused on the night's task. He was suddenly anxious. His poetic spirit would have to be replenished for he was tired from the day's work. The reality of being a poet hung about him like the stale cigarette smoke. One had to pull out new images every day – from somewhere. Even the nonsensical, the idiotic, the laughable. He'd done well on the first few rounds. He sensed the verses were well chosen, the rhythm clear and crisp, the impact felt. But laziness threatened to overtake him.

He started:

Special words, shapes, figures,
A new beginning lies in wait . . .

But these words came with difficulty. He had to go home and sleep off the night's work. He reached inside

MISBEGOTTEN

and pulled out the book of Cornelius's poetry that he'd already well dog-eared. Perhaps a little inspiration. He flipped to a random page.

He'd intended to depend on himself a bit longer but why labour with his own tired language? He'd wanted to woo her on his own terms, with his own images, words, rhyme. But why struggle? The poet's words would speak equally well for him. And to wear the poet's identity was to wear his tweedy, ageing good looks – to become a famous bard. And in becoming a famous bard, he would woo the fair lady. It was a heady, ancient plan.

This would be as good as anything he could muster. And now he would claim the verses of a famous poet for his gameplaying! Why not? If there was one thing easier than duping the world with poetry, it was duping the world with other people's poetry.

Like playing poker with counterfeit money: the stakes were reduced, the take greater.

But then an urge to do it himself consumed him. If he could do anything, then why not this? If he could perpetrate any con, he could surely handle the most basic one of all: a few words contrived together to alter someone's emotions. He was used to playing a part. He was used to phoney accents, fake beards and false papers. Poetry was all of those and yet less: just some sugary syllables sprinkled on a page to lure an unsuspecting sweet-tooth.

Inspired by the quiet of the taxi stand, he listened to his heart beat. His pulse, still pounding from the last con, tolled like a churchbell in a nearby parish. What was it that the poet had said? Write from experience? Ideas just roll along, he'd said, like a cab on a winter's night. Crapshoot lifted the pen and scrawled a few lines. They looked as good on the page as anything he had ever seen in the great book of Conan J. Cornelius.

He reread the last line with pleasure:

Leads to a loyalty so true.

Then as an afterthought, he added:

I dream of a son. How about you?

Crapshoot smiled at the final rhyme. More poets should learn their craft from him, he thought, on his walk to the mailbox. *Genius, pure genius.* The type of genius that always went unrecognised.
Until love, however misguided, claimed it.

23

'Dr Dotterweich will see you now.'

'Thank you.' Caitlin stood up and headed to the familiar office. The door opened and a hand ushered her to one of the high-backed guest chairs.

'Wonderful to see you, Mrs Bourke. I see that we *are* getting somewhere,' said Dotterweich smiling and nodding at her somewhat swollen belly.

'You have a good eye, Doctor. Paul noticed for the first time last night. And that was without my blouse.'

'I have a trained eye. A clinician's eye. Your husband has love's eye. And as you know quite well, love is often blind. It's sad – the myopia of true emotion. Science is so far-sighted in comparison. Yet there's something to be said for that old-fashioned lens.'

'I suppose.'

'Mrs Bourke, you are patient with my ramblings.'

'Indeed,' she said with Dotterweich's exact inflection.

'And you maintain a sense of humour. Wonderful. There is no better therapy for a healthy baby.'

'Baby?'

'Yes.'

'Can't you be more specific?'

'You *are* positive you want to know?'

'That's what I'm here for.' She was hardly patient with Dotterweich or his ramblings any more. Or with his pompous, pedantic tone. Or with his self-righteous theories. Or with his preaching. Or with anything. She just wanted to know.

She just wanted to know – for her and, more importantly, for *the father*. She carried around his poetry now, and she'd developed a small scrapbook. Some poems had gone there. Others had gone on the wall in the den for good luck.

'Well then, Mrs Bourke.' Dotterweich glanced down at his file to double-check the finding. 'You are the proud bearer of a beautiful, healthy, magnificent, baby: *a boy.*'

Caitlin closed her eyes and felt joy expand geometrically. To know the gender was to know so much more. To know that it was a boy was to know that it was human. And to know that it was human was to know what resided within her. Not animal. Not monstrosity. Not biological mistake.

But a human. A friend.

A son – her son.

His son.

24

Though he'd never been on a date, he knew what seduction required.

He'd seen movies. He'd even sipped red wine.

Crapshoot chose six different poems this time. Then he posted them. He enclosed a note: *I wrote these for you – and for us – all three of us.*

Seduction was to convince someone that you were what you were not. That was the simple equation he kept in his head as he drove about. A date was a performance. Each player acting – convincing the other that they were someone better than they were. He would be a famous poet, only to not be. Someone else might be suave or debonair, only to turn callous and slovenly along with the ringing of the wedding bells.

The element of seduction excited him. But as he approached the red light, he discovered that the seduction followed the rape: he had *penetrated* her – through a test tube, perhaps – but he *had still penetrated her*. And if she'd known him really, known his mind and his predilections, she'd never have consented. So it was rape, in the end. And a very high-tech rape at that. A test tube rape. He laughed. *A test tube rape.* He'd outdone himself.

He recalled the Northport whore who'd been dumped

in the Essex River. Crapshoot had driven by the riverside just as the police discovered the body. Her once human torso was badly mutilated and only the tangled spandex that vaguely imitated the pattern of arms gave the hint of what once was. Crapshoot got out of his cab to watch the paramedics load the remains in the ambulance. He heard a policeman say she'd probably been raped, then killed, then mutilated. So primitive, Crapshoot had thought: the rape ended with murder and the mutilation was a desperate attempt to inflict more pain, even after death. Such rage, so misguided. For to really rape, to really mutilate, necessitated keeping the body alive, maintaining a pulse, causing real agony to a real human form.

At the red light, he glanced in the rearview. He didn't look like a rapist. He didn't even look like a man with a cruel heart. *I am always in season*. Yes, he was playing a part all right. He laughed again.

Would that she would play hers.

25

Today he would meet her.

He was impatient with poetry. The construction of words was tedious. There was something so certain, so easy, about a fatal cut to the jugular, a wallet lifted, a job well done. The gnawing came along more and more often. And he would rest his palm lightly, just below the carnation, to slow its insistence. The intoxication of power over another was what brought it on. Perhaps it was fatherhood. He had never been father before. Fatherhood. Maybe that was it.

Today he would meet her.

This he was thinking as he drove down the Merritt Parkway, enjoying the breezes. Connecticut beckoned to him in springtime. With a certain type of indistinct longing, he noticed the botanical changes, the magic of the thaw, the way music on his car radio sounded better with the windows down.

Springtime made him feel like shopping.

Let's go shopping, he said under his breath, the Range Rover maintaining a steady fifty-five a few yards in front of him.

She was pretty, he thought. With springtime, her stomach had swelled. Not so noticeably that anyone would see without looking closely, but he was not just anyone. She looked healthy, maternal – at least to him. Her blonde hair she'd cut to a bob. In the Range Rover, suspended above the cars around her, Caitlin Bourke looked happy.

The exit. The off-ramp. The circling round and round. The turnoff into the mall.

Let's go shopping.

Crapshoot waited silently, counting the shoppers, the shops, the minutes, the dollars in his pocket. Then Caitlin emerged from the Toy Park toting a bag of goodies – all manner of playthings. The items were spilling sublimely from her shopping bags: he imagined the games, stuffed animals, Barbie dolls, Ken dolls, and everything else that could buy happiness in a child. Crapshoot watched her struggle with the bags, the toys, the big piles of fun.

A child's world was such simplicity, thought Crapshoot. A Dacron bear, a tricycle, a puzzle – any one of these things could produce a world unto itself, a place of fascination, a potion for the imagination.

Joy.

But the things that made a parent happy were so complicated – the result of perfect hormonal alignments, tenuous emotional equilibria, turgid passions. Caitlin, for example, needed a baby to make her happy. Crapshoot considered the complexity that such a tall order required: the genetic matching, the cellular divisions, the neurodevelopment, the right piece of such and such at this and that time.

It seemed impossible.

While he, Crapshoot, needed so very little. He was like a child in his demands: money, power, a little bit of cruelty.

And Caitlin would make him happy. She would start

MISBEGOTTEN

today. A happy family, meeting for the first time. It was not the traditional way, of course. Tradition would have to wait.

He drove alongside the Range Rover and looked about. No one seemed to notice him in the sea of cars and shopping plans. But then one woman tried to flag him down and he flicked on the off-duty light, doubtful it would hold its own against the sunshine. She waddled away with her bags and headed for the pay phone and he relaxed again.

Crapshoot parked nearby and walked to Caitlin's Range Rover. After a quick glance around, he popped the hood and disconnected the battery connectors. He slammed back the hood, returned to his cab and waited.

A Barbie doll, a Ken doll – simplicity – the little things in life . . .

He adjusted his carnation once again: it was an important day.

26

Pausing in the parking lot with the two shopping bags weighing her down equally on either side, Caitlin had a moment of not remembering where the car was. There were so many Range Rovers in Connecticut these days and they were all green. But then she remembered the general direction and headed that way.

The sunlight was blinding and the reflection of dozens of auto tops set about her head like a suburban kaleidoscope of many colours. She was happy with the day and the shopping. Knowing that *he* would be a boy was to know what to do. She felt she now knew everything he would ever need. These toys, those clothes, this love, that maternity. Buying the toys was fun. The store aisles, so full of promise, had spilled into one another. There were so many things that she could imagine giving him. How joyful it would make her feel to give him things.

She loaded the happy heft of the bags into the Range Rover and turned the ignition. It groaned and she tried again. And again. The groan of the car melted into her own. She exhaled in frustration. She'd never had this problem and she sat bolt upright in the comfortable seat and cursed that she hadn't installed a cellular phone. She checked the headlights but the toggle switch sat in its proper position. Caitlin looked around for a sign of salvation. There was a pay phone across the parking lot. That would be the thing to do. She could call the auto club; she was a member. Paul had told her many times that calling the auto club would get you a quick tow and a ride to wherever you were going. She searched for the phone number in her pocketbook and was struck by a moment of self-pity that coincided with the throb of the baby inside her. It didn't matter what Paul said about these things. Paul had always given her the advice: *you call the auto club, that's what you do*. She could hear those irritating tones which he got in his voice when he was self-assured about something petty. But the baby could not look to Paul. The baby would look to her. After all, she had to protect *him*. She searched more quickly in her bag. She didn't like the feeling of being in a shopping mall and unable to leave.

No, the baby could not look to Paul. He was no more to the baby than this cab driver who was motioning her to roll down her window.

She tried to open it, but then laughed at herself: the electronic window was as dead as the rest of the Range Rover. She opened the door ajar.

'Yes?'

'Is your battery dead?'

'I think so.' She looked at the man sitting bolt upright in the driver seat of the cab. He was unusually dressed. She couldn't help but notice the well-pressed suit, the flower in the lapel, the overly formal gestures and the cultivated voice.

'Yes, I think I passed by your jeep a little earlier and you'd left the lights on.'

'Oh, I don't think so. I checked – '

'Of course, you checked the switch. In the Range Rovers,

MISBEGOTTEN

the auto lights malfunction, go on and then don't go off. It's not your fault. I've seen many of these British bugs, and that's the way it goes. Of course, I can give you a ride, to wherever, as long as it's not too far. To a gas station or a tow lot. I won't charge you. I have sympathy for travellers in distress.'

He smiled expansively and Caitlin felt better. This would be easier than calling the auto club and waiting for however long. She could get a ride to a tow service and then just hire them back to the mall. But if it was only the battery ... 'Could you just give me a jump start? I mean, do you have cables? That would be the easiest. And I'd be glad to pay you for it. Say, twenty dollars?'

The cab driver looked disappointed. He sat silent for a moment, evidently trying to remember whether he had jump cables, and then opened his door and came around to her window. He smiled again. He had an electric smile. It exposed large, white teeth. But there was something mildly unnatural about it. Something – not phoney – but too *genuine*. 'I absolutely will try that. I always forget that I have cables in my trunk. And I won't even charge you.' He raised his palm quickly to derail any protest. 'Now, like I said before, a traveller in distress – and an expectant mother, at that.'

Caitlin immediately looked down. She hadn't known it was that obvious yet. She knew her belly had swollen, but to be tagged as a mother that way ... Well, she would be proud, now that it had happened. 'Yes, not too much longer now.' She laughed. 'I was doing a little shopping. Toys and things. It's fun to stock up in advance.' What a gauche comment if she hadn't been pregnant. It was a golden rule never to ask someone if they were pregnant, if you weren't sure. How that could lead to an awkward moment –

'Of course.' His voice was all she could follow, now that he'd propped open the hood and stretched out the jump cables and had bent down to fiddle with the connections. She found herself worrying that he might dirty his suit. It was odd that he was dressed so formally. She looked at the cab door – NORTHPORT TAXI – maybe they had very stringent dress codes for their drivers. Or maybe he was headed to a wedding. She wasn't thinking straight: a wave of nausea passed and she closed her eyes to quell it. 'Well, I think I have the connection straight now. Why don't you try starting her up?'

Caitlin tried the ignition. It started without hesitation. The quiet purr of the foreign engine was a welcome sound. 'Thank you,' she called. 'That's a relief.' She reached into her handbag to get out a $20 bill. It was only right. But he was already at her window, shaking his head.

'Now that would be rude, wouldn't it, after I told you that I'm charitable to travellers in distress.'

'It was kind of you,' she said embarrassedly and put her pocketbook on the passenger seat. 'Well, thank you. Thank you very much.'

She waited for him to remove his arm from the door so she could finally close it. But his hand remained fixed, fingering the rubber that ran along the top of the window frame. 'Is it a boy or a girl?'

It seemed a strange question, given that most people don't usually know, and although she *did* know, she all of a sudden didn't want to tell him.

'I don't know. Best to keep that a surprise.'

He smiled. She was disturbed by the smile. It seemed to know that she was lying. Another wave of nausea passed, followed by a slight chill. She hoped she wasn't getting sick. It was time to go home.

'Aren't you delighted to be on the threshold of giving

birth?' he asked, the smile fading. 'I mean it is a thrill, I imagine. It's not so easy to impregnate these days. You're fortunate to be fertile. Make the most of it. There's a lot of worry out there, I know. There's a lot to shield the young ones from these days. You see, I understand what you're going through. I, too, am – '

'I'm sorry.' It was time to go. She didn't want to be rude, but she was feeling ill and she didn't have time to talk with a stranger and have strange conversations. It was easy enough to tolerate the most unbearable social penance when feeling well. But with a dose of sickness, the smallest exchange of words was an ordeal. Caitlin studied the man's face. He was frowning. She felt some guilt now along with the nausea. Clearly he was lonely. 'I'm not feeling well. And I have a long ride back home. Thank you very much for your help.'

Again the all-too-genuine smile. 'It won't take you long to Westbridge on a Saturday, fifteen minutes tops.'

'Right, thanks again.' She slammed the door shut and pulled into the lanes of the parking lot, blending quickly with the other exiting cars. She felt a sense of relief. She wasn't sure why. As she rolled round and round and on to the highway, she opened the window and let the fresh air wash with the sun along her cheek. She felt the nausea pass. It was good to be on the highway moving quickly after all that time sitting still. There was very little traffic. He was right ... *It won't take you long to Westbridge on a Saturday, fifteen minutes tops* ... She remembered the suit, the knowing smile, the flower in the lapel. He was a strange man ... *won't take you long to Westbridge* ... How did he know she was from Westbridge?

She cocked her head, as if to hear a distant noise. I guess it's not too hard to figure out that a Range Rover around here is going to Westbridge, she thought, feeling a sense of embarrassed nakedness at being so easily pegged for her wealth. The awkward feeling stayed a few minutes but then she regained the former elation at her purchases, and it pushed any memory of the cab driver far from her mind.

27

He was back in school. School had always bored him: the claptrap of teachers speaking from behind a mouldy desk, the rules and regulations that didn't let anyone do anything worth doing. He had always skipped school anyway, so his memories couldn't be trusted. Most of his ideas of school came from the TV that he watched while he was skipping school. So, with a sudden pang of fierce justice, Crapshoot decided it really was not fair for him to judge.

But this school would be different. He had never been to a birthing school and he had no idea of the curriculum. He imagined some words of advice on childbearing and rearing, followed by some homilies on family life. Whatever would come he was ready for: he was always fond of new experiences.

He was always in season.

And, of course, *she* would be there.

A few mothers had already entered the room, pulling small mats from a stack near the back wall and assembling them in a circle in the centre. One father came on the heels of his wife and sat next to her, looking done in by the day's work – uncomfortable and self-conscious in his business clothes. Crapshoot laughed softly: he would not be the only suit. He immediately felt a disdain for this middle-class banker-father who had been shunted to this place by his domineering wife. The sorry man would till the corporate soil for his family like a Russian serf and develop ulcers and glaucoma in the shadow of their patronage. And then he would die, leaving behind a legacy no more impressive than his retirement account and his lime green bedroom slippers.

A matronly woman he assumed was the teacher took a neutral position at the head of the circle, marking her authority only by the way she sat, absolutely self-assured, in a yogic style, surveying the room with open ears and closed eyes.

There was still no sign of Caitlin. He wondered how she would dress. Ever since the exchange outside the Toy Park, he'd developed a fixed image which he knew was flawed. The first up-close encounter never presents a complete picture. He had trouble visualising the curve of her pregnancy – the silhouette of the belly that indicated the shape of the new generation. And *that* was what he wanted to see. In the nourishing, bright sunlight of that brief encounter, a dark emotion had taken seed. He'd looked at the belly and realised that something of *his* resided there. In a surge of possessive lust, he decided that he would have his property. After all, property was property and his was his. He was never one to part with his property. In the living – the flesh and the blood – he had never before seen anything he really wanted. All his wants were inanimate: a spanking new car, a fat wallet, a five-bedroom house, or glittering gold. The only thing organic in his midst was the fresh carnation that sat routinely on the threshold of his heart – where the gnawing today, as nearly every day now, seized him mercilessly.

But he *would* have that which was rightfully his.

MISBEGOTTEN

A woman to his left gestured towards him to come and sit on the mat. 'Don't be afraid to sit in the circle. Really. We won't bite. The instructor – Alexa – is very nice and very understanding,' she said, her pregnancy looking ominously large against her small form. She must have been in the home stretch. Crapshoot slipped off the small stool and sat on a mat next to the disproportional mother-to-be. 'I see you've just come from work.' She waved at his suit. 'A lot of dads do that, and of course moms too, so don't be the least bit self-conscious about it. Is your wife here?'

'No, I mean, we're not married. And she's not here. It looks like I'm the representative.' He smiled his broadest smile.

'That's fine. We have many untraditionals here. I'm a single mother myself. And we get many fathers – usually.' She looked with disappointment around the room. 'Mondays are tough for fathers. It's Mondays when we state our regrets. Men have trouble stating their regrets.'

'I see.'

His attention was wandering now, considering Caitlin and the baby and wondering why she hadn't yet shown. By intercepting her mail, he knew she'd signed up for the class. He did not imagine she was one to be late for things. A growing scorn grew in him for the woman to his left. She droned on in her well-practised way.

And then Caitlin arrived.

She was noticeably pregnant and Crapshoot felt a possessiveness grip him as he watched her settle into a cross-legged position four places to his right. His view was slightly obscured. She smiled in turn at the others in the circle and she clearly knew them by sight if not by name. When her gaze reached him, she smiled too, but uncomfortably as if she felt sorry for not remembering a familiar face. He stared at her, the gnawing in his heart increasing, and wondered if she remembered him, but her quick attention to the rest of the group told him that she didn't.

'Deep breathing,' began Alexa, holding her palms out on the imaginary plane of the faces in front of her and beginning a long inhalation.

Crapshoot didn't participate, but instead watched the others, including the insubstantial father, perform the exercise. He imagined the weak ways in which they would rear their young, prepping them with silly instruction, coddling their worst indulgences – giving them a sorry chance of surviving in the new world. Looking out at the multitude of upraised palms in front of him was like looking at the empty hands of a thousand crippled beggars, all entreating him for a handout of some kind. This was the kind of culture he despised.

The woman to his left fingered his elbow to scold him. He instinctively shrank away, shielding his concealed, shoulder-holstered gun from her touch. 'You have to do the breathing,' she whispered. 'Without the breathing, nothing else will follow. The breathing is the key. It releases the everyday tension and allows for the circulation to open up. And from there you can get the awareness of your surroundings. From there you can relax enough to state your regrets, and that brings honesty. And that honesty ... that honesty is what will help baby most of all.'

He decided to ignore her. Someone had turned down the lights and now the circle resembled a seance. He would have preferred a bit of pagan ritual: some blood from the womb, a bonfire in the middle, a child sacrifice on the fringe. But a seance. He laughed inwardly at the thought of it: raising the living from the wombs. It was appropriate. It might as well have been the dead. Those unfortunate growths that rested in those swollen maternal bellies were no more suited to this world than spirits from the beyond. Crapshoot had no interest in any of them, disdained them all. Except one ...

He looked at Caitlin, eyes closed, palms outstretched, her belly distended. There was a special something *there* at least. Something that belonged to him.

The voice of Alexa interrupted: 'And slowly, slowly open, slowly ... OK.' All had opened their eyes but the lights remained dim. 'It's Monday. So it's time for regrets. For newcomers, this is a way to let baby come into the world uncluttered by our shortcomings. We say our regrets so that baby will never have to. We all come to this with some regrets, and to be honest we have to share them. It's not honest to pretend that birth is perfect.' She looked at the ceiling. 'It's only honest to be aware of our weaknesses.'

'How about you?' she began with a nondescript older mother who was still rail thin. 'Will you begin for us, Melanie?'

Melanie looked pleased to be asked. Crapshoot flashed her a menacing grin. She looked down and spoke mumblingly into the carpet. 'I still regret what I regretted last week: waiting so late to give birth. It's not that I had much trouble. Luckily we were able to conceive like that.' She snapped her fingers, but they were too weak to make a sound. Someone giggled. Alexa smiled encouragingly. Melanie continued but her voice was even smaller and Crapshoot struggled to hear the dim words. It was pitiful, he thought, to listen to this refuse. They would all do better to spend a night on the street, seeing what was real. 'That was a blessing. I'm forty, though,' her voice started to break. The tears began to come. 'And I don't know what kind of health I'll be in when he graduates from college, when he gets married. Will I ever see his grandchildren?'

'So state the regret,' Alexa intervened.

She struggled with the tears, now falling freely. A disembodied hand offered a tissue. 'The regret is that I started this all too late . . .' The dike burst, the tissue was useless now.

They all sat in the relative darkness, absorbing her sobs. Crapshoot listened closely. The sound of another's pain was often a comfort to him. He relished the sound of the whip of his pistol breaking a jaw. Or the agonised fear in the desperation of a voice that begged him to show mercy. Pain was a part of life. Pain was a part of the world of commerce: there was no pleasure of triumph without someone else's corresponding pain of defeat. A buck more in someone's hands was a buck less in another's. When treasure changes hands, one suffers, the other rejoices. That's what economics was all about. The pirates knew it as well as anyone. And the sound of another's pain – he relished that like the jingling of change in his own pocket.

'And you, Caitlin? How about your regrets?'

Alexa waited patiently as Caitlin gathered her thoughts. What could she have to regret? thought Crapshoot, staring at the face that had worn a little thin with loneliness and fatigue. She was having his baby, after all.

'I regret hurting Paul,' she began, the words halting in a dry throat. A hand offered a cup of water. 'Thank you. I mean this is not his baby, and I wonder about the pain of that.' She hesitated, as if to make a true confession, and closed her eyes at the discomfort of it. Alexa nodded – a nod of understanding that announced knowledge of the whole situation – and sat at attention. 'I feel a closeness to the real father and I regret that and feel guilty about that.

MISBEGOTTEN

I don't know the real father but I feel I know him.' She pointed to her belly. 'There's something here that says I know him. And I really don't want to hurt Paul. Paul has never been a good husband, but he could've been a good father. Now I guess he'll be neither. I feel sorry for him.' She didn't cry. Her voice cracked but the tears did not come. Crapshoot admired her toughness. What strong will it was to discuss this among all of these strangers. And in front of him. 'It's hard. He's a bastard and here I am alone with my baby and myself. I sometimes think it's all a big mistake.' Then she smiled: 'But then again, I love this child. And he's all mine to love.'

Alexa reached over to touch Caitlin's hand. The insignificant father sighed with sympathy.

Crapshoot clenched his fist in silent anger. It was not *all hers* to love. It was, more than anyone's, *his*. The infernal ingratitude of those who took their grub and walked away without thanking the hand that fed them. Like welfare bums on the dole, not making a living and cursing the state, Caitlin sat there and labelled her belly all her own.

'And you? You're new to our group, are you not? If you feel comfortable, please go ahead and join in.'

Crapshoot looked up. Alexa was talking to him. Caitlin now looked in his direction and he thought he noticed a slight recognition in the way she pulled closer to the circle.

'I will, thank you.' Crapshoot felt very conscious of playing his part. He would now play the expectant father: sensitive, demonstrative, contrite – happy. It was a real challenge. For although he was an expectant father, he was not the least bit contrite. He was hateful and the eyes focused upon him made him more and more hateful. But the game was his. He was in his element. This was the way all great cons began – with a bit of hate, a bit of luck, and a glint in the eye.

I am always in season.

'I regret not having come sooner to this very, very important group.' There were murmurs of appreciation and agreement. He waited, with the skill of a seasoned speaker, for a solemn silence to return. 'The mother of my child is a wonderful woman: generous, kind, strong. She is here in spirit, I'm sure. I regret that I am not as much the father as I should be. I hope to play more of a role as time goes by. That's why I've come here.' He looked directly at Caitlin but she was looking at the carpet. The insignificant father smiled. The woman to his left touched him affectionately on the lower arm. Alexa said in a cloying tone: 'Thank you. We welcome you to the group.'

As the meeting disbanded, Crapshoot tried to catch Caitlin in the foyer. She was quick out the door and he walked briskly to overtake her. He wanted to be near her and to see her up close. He'd even wished to touch her belly – to touch that which was his. But she was very fast, despite her new weight, and the woman to his left waylaid him as they reached the elevator.

'Really, you don't have to regret not coming here sooner. You made the right decision by coming tonight. No time is ever lost among people who care.' She had her hand again on his elbow as the two of them watched the crowded elevator close on Caitlin and his child and the others. He caught Caitlin's eye just as the door slammed shut. 'We'll catch the next one. You know what they say: there'll always be another bus.'

Crapshoot stared at the woman's chubby face. It was the face of a mother, with the luminous optimism of those months and the patience of a hundred others.

'I thank you for your kindness.'

'Please,' she looked delighted at his encouraging

response. 'No need to thank. This isn't about thanks. This is about parenthood – something bigger than any of us.'

Crapshoot noticed her elegant jade necklace, overly fancy for a birthing class. It looked real. There was a very plump diamond ring on her wedding finger. Even before he'd seen them, he knew what he would do.

'I thought you said you were single?'

'Oh that,' she said, proudly extending her knuckle. 'That's a ring of the vow I took with myself. I thought it important to mark the vow of my commitment – to my child, I mean – with a sort of symbol. I guess it's a wedding of a type.'

They entered the elevator. When the door closed, they were alone. One fluorescent in the elevator flickered out and they were left in shadows. The mother gazed up at Crapshoot and looked as if she'd just seen him for the first time, and was noticing the stiff suit, the carnation, the odd, amused smile.

He relished the look: in it was a certain fear – the fear of having made a miscalculation, or of having left something entirely out of the equation. He was reminded of the look in the eyes of any victim as the reality of the con begins to dawn: the eyes of a carjack victim as the gun appears, the eyes of a three card monte dupe when the red queen doesn't.

The elevator was slow to move and for a moment there was the strange sensation that they might be stuck. They looked at each other and the mother looked away. When it finally descended, Crapshoot heard her breathe again with relief. The doors opened and she exited first. She wished him a rushed farewell and headed for her car in the dark lot. He made a point of wishing her a demonstrative goodbye in front of the balding, inattentive security guard. Then he headed for his cab that was parked out on the main street, while she walked in the other direction to the lot. As soon as he reached the street, he circled back down the alley that ran along the building and re-emerged in the parking lot on the other side. By now, everyone had gone and there was a quiet bleakness to the abandoned lot, with just her Mercedes sitting on the fresh asphalt. She moved quickly. Then she looked back once, nearly tripping on an abandoned can, and he was close on her heels. She looked at him as though he might have forgotten something but her look of inquiry turned to a frown as she sensed an equation out of balance. *Smart woman,* thought Crapshoot. The lot was empty and her last look clinched the bargain – it was definitely the look of a victim when the con is up. He was putting on his gloves. There was no way out after that look.

He reached her just as she put the key in her car. *I am always in season.* His hand shot out like a comet and whipped her face with the pistol butt and she fell. He stifled the scream with his gloved hand, but she was still with him, fully conscious, and gazing up at him in groggy fear. His hand slipped and she screamed in a limp voice that barely reached above the din of the nearby highway exit, 'The, the baby ... please ... my baby,' but he raised the pistol high and came crashing down with medieval strength, crushing the base of her neck against the pavement. He could take no chances with this one. He pulled away from the body and noticed he'd soiled his jacket with blood. After reproaching himself for his sloppiness, he got in his cab and drove it under the highway and into the train station lot where it wouldn't be noticed until he picked it up tomorrow. Then he walked briskly back to the Mercedes. All was quiet now. He started up the car, and then got out again and looked at the large torso. He

MISBEGOTTEN

removed his jacket, his tie, his holster, his shirt. He gave a swift, massively violent kick to the swollen belly. Then he took a plastic bag from the trunk and busied himself on the asphalt with a knife and the bag. It was messy work and he would have to dispose of his pants.

As he drove away in the Mercedes, he admired his deft fingers and thought with pleasure of his trophy. Everything was potentially his property: it was only a matter of claiming it.

28

'This is *lunatic*!'

'Perhaps.'

'Perhaps?! Shit! This is *absolutely* nuts!'

'Sit down, Serena. I'll fix you a drink.'

'Good, I need it.' She looked at her watch. 'Even if it is only noon. And you, honey, need something much stronger than a drink.'

Caitlin left to get the whiskey and Serena scanned the den walls: poetry pasted there, the lines and lines of verses, the words looming unsteadily, a testimonial to something very bizarre.

Caitlin returned with the drinks. 'They make me happy.'

'I'll bet. Does Paul know about this?'

'No. He never comes in here. And even if he did, he wouldn't know what to make of it. I guess I leave it up partly as a rebuke. I'm half waiting for him to say something.'

'And just who is *he* exactly?'

'I don't know, but clearly someone special . . . someone gifted . . . someone sensitive.'

'And clearly a nut.'

'I've read every word he sends me. He understands the

spirit. Paul can't even understand the philosophy on a fortune cookie. What other choice do I have?'

Serena sat and swigged. 'You can get a hold of yourself.'

'Serena, he talks about me – about our child, about hope, about the magical, the poetic. Do you understand? This could be my only chance.'

'What is this? Do you plan to run away with this poet?!'

Caitlin hadn't really expected Serena to understand. Not that she really understood herself. But Serena had clearly misinterpreted. It was not a relationship like that. It was cerebral, otherworldly. For her, the poems were a way out. In each verse was an answer. In the collection was a prayer. In the body of work was a revelation.

The closeness she felt to this mysterious father was akin to the closeness she felt to her similarly mysterious child. With the movements in her belly which of late were so palpable that they foretold something absolutely original. To do everything with another soul had made her fearful at first – as though the slightest misstep would take not one, but two. Yet the promise of another being to help her, someone who could take responsibility for the magic that resided within her, converted fear into power.

She had read *his* words. He had a way of putting words together that replaced the words with feeling. When the house was silent at night she'd taken to locking herself in the den and studying a verse. When she read it, she heard *his* voice read – a steady, authoritative voice that filled the big house with airy images. There was a harmony between the rhythm of her womb and the poems.

She realised that he was still wholly anonymous to her. A name, perhaps, would make a difference. But it was other things, small things that intrigued: what he liked for breakfast, or what he watched on TV – if he watched TV.

MISBEGOTTEN

She imagined what he did as he wrote: whether he smoked a pipe (as she had often pictured) or just took strong coffee, or perhaps a bath afterwards or a shower before. As she read his carefully crafted expressions of redemption, she wondered too what he thought of her, what he wanted to express to her, what he wanted from their child. Once she found herself speculating on his past romances, and then quickly dismissed the thought as childish: what did she care for his past dalliances; she was not seeking a mate but a sire.

There was something primeval about the relationship, just as Dotterweich suggested. She felt a pure romance that derived from the biological connection. If she'd met him on a blind date in a Parisian bistro she would surely have hated him, found him pretentious, self-absorbed, paternalistic. If he'd lecherously approached her in a piano bar, she would have felt nauseated, dirty – wanted for the wrong reasons. If she'd taken a course with him as professor, she would have scorned his arrogance. But that he'd hopped over these sadly modern forms of social interaction and injected himself as pure biology into her womb – with absolute anonymity – guaranteed that he would find a way into her heart.

She admitted to herself that fantasy was contained in vagueness. Not knowing all his predilections, all his whimsies – even his name – was more fun than knowing them. Not having any idea of what his skin smelled like in bed or the rhythm of his breathing during orgasm was a blissful ignorance. Knowing not at all his facial features or his choice of after-dinner drink was a cause for miraculous excitement. Void of insight into the chaos of his morning routine or the dull torpor of his afternoon naps, he found herself more drawn to him. Without an inkling of whether he let Crest congeal on the sides of the sink or assiduously sloshed it into the plumbing after brushing, she experienced an insatiable affinity with his spirit. She felt undeniably drawn towards his smoky aloofness and lack of person.

Not knowing him, she loved him.

Anonymity had always excited her. As a teenager she'd had a recurring fantasy that took place on a transatlantic ocean liner. After her parents had stowed her in her own cabin and gone for drinks in the lounge, she crawled into bed and waited. Soon there was an instant darkness in the room and the feel of hands gently rising under her blouse. Her lover was kind, supple, strong and invisible. His hands were specially suited to his task and his breathing was in time with hers. After some time, the span of which she couldn't possibly determine, he left her and she drifted into sleep. At dinner the next night, as the guests all sat genteelly around dinner tables and made sophisticated conversation, she wondered which of the many handsome men present was her lover. She knew that he was there, somewhere in the stateroom, somewhere dining, somewhere plotting the next visit. Identification impossible, she resigned herself again to the nightly intrigue and dutifully waited for the lights to dim. Night after night, the pattern repeated itself, she never getting any closer to his identity, he never revealing himself by any daylight sign.

This was a fantasy that relied on anonymity. Yet she had to know that he was present somewhere on the ship. If she imagined the fantasy shoreside and pictured herself waiting in a house at night for an unknown lover to creep through the window, the excitement vanished into fear and loathing. What excited her was the containment of the space, the knowledge that he was there, the impossibility of finding him. Any setting that afforded the same peculiar blend of security and anonymity could elicit the same passion on her part.

With *him*, there was a similar reliance on anonymity, on the not knowing that served as inspiration. By reading his poems, she gleaned the desired effect. Through the poems she could traverse his world but not his space, probe his celestial thoughts but never his mundane habits, know him completely but not at all.

'I said, are you going to figure out who he is? Are you going to run away with this guy?' Serena slipped off her heels, sank into the couch and held the whiskey high in her hand like Lady Liberty.

Caitlin looked at Serena. Two more whiskeys and she would understand perfectly. Which was worse: a fantasy built around the bottle or around a test tube? 'Of course not.'

'Then what? What's this about?'

'I don't know.'

'You don't know?'

'I don't know.'

And though she didn't, she felt that just as in a fantasy, she would know what to do when the lights finally dimmed.

'How can you not know?'

'How can I? This isn't about any reality. This isn't taught in school – or at the altar. I have no idea what's going on. But this is the most *interested* I've ever been. In *anyone*.'

'What about me, darling?' Serena joked flirtatiously, sucking her fingertip of a drop of whiskey.

'I've never been much interested in you at all, Serena.'

'Nor I you, lover girl,' said Serena, now getting her noontime buzz. 'You know what? I say you're a sorry romantic.'

'Serena, I gave up on fairy tales a long time ago. This is beyond that.'

'Oh, it's a fairy tale, all right. But I'd watch out if I were you. You know what they say about fairy tales? They're really very scary, gory, ugly stories about evil and madness. Not really for children.'

'What's scary is that they sometimes come true,' replied Caitlin, closing her eyes.

29

Like an appraiser at an estate sale, he took a methodical inventory. But the household smells were not of the stale residue of death and a life lived; instead he sensed a life about to be.

In the entry foyer, where he was careful not to track in any dirt, Crapshoot noted the large fashionable mahogany pieces and the original art. Though it was dark and his knowledge of painting limited, he sensed that the frames contained large oils of some repute. Certainly, they were more than prints. He imagined them to be Old Masters, convinced that such paintings would command such majestic frames.

Having had some trouble with the alarm, he took time to make sure it was disarmed before gathering his tools and placing them in his small satchel. Then he let his eyes adjust to the light. The stairs were richly carpeted, expansive, up the landing in a voluptuous style and to the second floor. More paintings lined this space and tempted his acquisitive eye, but he checked the rashness of that impulse and thought of greater possessions.

Instead of heading up the stairs, he passed left into the living room, a palatial space with tasteful, contemporary furnishings and a stately grand piano. There were large, intricate sculptures of brass and clay and large vases of fresh lilies throughout. Crapshoot smiled. An appraiser's dream. Compulsively he began to record each item in his mind's eye, more for the purposes of an obscure and sinewy pleasure than for any practical purpose. To mentally tag each item was a prelude to ownership. With time it could all be his: the paintings, the home, the sculptures.

He could remove their ownership instantly, through theft, fancy or artistry, while they would continue to cling to legal principles that defined the rights of ownership – useless abstract notions of what belongs to whom, unbuttressed by might or right or anything in between.

But he wanted more than even that.

Off the living room was a small den, much warmer and more personable than the living room. A single lamp with a rice-paper shade had been left on and the light cast shadows which leaked along the wall of bookshelves. It was many seconds spent observing the choice of books and the various personal items – photos assembled in montages in frames, blue knitting left hastily on the couch, a sole running sneaker somehow abandoned in a corner – before Crapshoot noticed the décor which graced the far wall. He approached the pages pasted there with a mere inquisitiveness, but after reading a bit and recognising some of the notes he'd sent, interspersed with Xeroxes of poems, he smiled appreciatively.

There, on that den wall, was his power and he stared at it as one might stare at an embarrassment of riches.

Make the sucker feel special.

He had made her feel special, indeed. So special that there, on her walls, she'd placed him as a shrine to the part he was playing. The effect of all this on his ego was not small and he couldn't help but rotate in a swoon of pleasure as he looked again at the poems and the letters.

He paused to read and found a bit of himself:

You and I
Poetry in motion
A biological link.
Our identities mere whispers
Only after dark.

Like the image of the red queen flickering hopelessly through the deck, these letters and poems foretold a great surprise. The gap between illusion – the red queen presenting herself at regular intervals, appearing to glide into the right place at the right time – and reality – the red queen sadly emerging as a black jack – was so vast that Crapshoot had to chuckle.

Make the sucker feel special. And she felt so special. That was clear.

He'd come to her house that night to catalogue her possessions, her wealth, her means, her soul and spirit. And to see where his newest possession, the newborn weary head, would rest. But he'd gotten so much more: a catalogue of her desires. This was the real prize – to know that he'd succeeded.

When he'd approached the house earlier that fertile June night, with the Westbridge evening air floating on the wings of opulent promise in that way that summer evenings in rich suburbs have, he'd been extremely careful and quiet. Crouching silently in the grove of trees that bordered the front lawn, he'd waited patiently, not necessarily expecting anything. Crapshoot had read that the annual Westbridge Heritage Ball was being held that night at the Westbridge Repertory Theater. He'd correctly gambled on the grip of that peculiar social function to allow him an undisturbed visit to the Bourke household. And when the opportunity presented itself with Caitlin emerging from the house, elegantly appointed in a maternity evening gown that highlighted her by now swollen womb, Paul close in tow, Crapshoot had finally allowed himself to breathe. And then he waited for the Range Rover to usher the couple along the gravel and out the drive and up to the main road. And only then did he approach the house, mindful of all the tasks he would have to accomplish in such a small time.

Now that he was successful and stood at the inner mantle of her private fixation, he only felt his greed swell. Why not have this house and all inside it? By all rights he owned her – her mind, passions, predilections. It seemed only logical that he should go upstairs and try on all her husband's suits, relax in a bubble bath, pour some wine – watch TV. He could fix himself a light supper in the kitchen or just dance happily on the Spanish tiled floor. Given the inclination, he might sample the colognes on the marble bathroom basin or light a fire in the living-room hearth.

On the way upstairs, he tagged and catalogued with greater conviction: this painting, that urn, the grandfather clock on the landing, an armoire in the upstairs foyer. He cursed his inability to label each with an exact dollar value. To tabulate the riches and reduce them to a comfortable sum would have given him great pleasure. As it was, he contented himself with a general sense of prosperity. A prosperity that would soon be his.

Off the upstairs hall, he entered a smaller room. A simple Shaker-style rocking chair with a blue needlepoint pillow sat unnaturally still in a corner. By the light of his

MISBEGOTTEN

small penlight, he could make out the wallpaper's powder blue hue and the mobiles swinging at the ready. Bright, pastel posters hung at appropriate intervals along the wall: something with elephants, another with Curious George. A stuffed bunny and several friends nestled comfortably in the corner of the crib. The hardwood floor was draped with a plush throw rug that featured the letters of the alphabet in multicolour. A compact changing table was placed next to the rocking chair. There was something missing. The absence puzzled him until he realised that there was nowhere to sleep: a crib would surely soon be placed in the patch empty of furnishings under the mobile.

Crapshoot adjusted his carnation and smiled. So this was the future home of the child-king. The wretched distillation of his slipshod sperm would sleep here! With Curious George and this beast of a bunny would his illegitimate son carouse! What paradise! To think of his offspring – his accursed layer of genetic froth – reclining here, in a crib, happily, without a care! On this changing table would his royal diapers be changed. In this rocking chair would his grievances be silenced with a suckle. With those mobiles would his newborn senses be stimulated and cajoled. And all until he was claimed by his owner.

Crapshoot revelled in this. Here, in the small room with the big plans, would come to rest his greatest possession. The paintings and the urns and the grandfather clocks were nothing in comparison to this, his greatest hold on *her*: the child.

His child.

Crapshoot felt the familiar gnawing in his heart and the throbbing in his groin. He lay on his back in the spot assigned for the crib, directly under the gently swinging mobile. He slipped a hand down to his pants, undid the zipper and reached inside. In a short while he felt his body buck with pleasure.

In the dark of the child's room, without the light of his penlight, was a blackness that abandoned the walls and the posters and the mobiles – a darkness which matched his soul.

30

A little girl held the quarter with care, walked with small child strides to the machine and turned the aluminium handle. A metallic cluck marked the gumball's arrival and the girl quickly retrieved it to pop it in her mouth. Caitlin watched the tiny ritual with interest and vaguely wondered where the mother was. But then the mother swooped down, *'I told you not before dinner!'* and rushed the daughter out of the store and into a waiting car. That was the kind of mother she didn't want to be, Caitlin thought, watching the car speed out of the parking lot and into the suburban traffic. Gumballs after dinner, homework before TV, wash the dishes, make the bed, brush the teeth. These were the things Caitlin didn't want to preach about. She'd had enough of boring routine in her life. Her child wouldn't have to suffer it too.

Passion, love, poetry: these were the things which would guide her son instead.

Caitlin, stimulated by the array of shapes and colours, walked past the row of cribs. Though there were interesting designs – some avant-garde, some hip, some industrial – Caitlin knew she wanted sheer tradition: a standard white crib which she could clutter up with fun pillows and animals. She stood in front of one that fitted her image, except that it was blue, and tried to picture her young son there, sated and snug, cosily nuzzling in the corner.

'Are you interested in that one?'

She answered the deep, salesman-like voice without turning. 'Maybe, but I really wanted it in white. I imagine you have the same one in white?'

'Oh, I don't work here,' the voice answered. 'I'm a parent-to-be: just shopping like you. I was also thinking of this one – in white.'

Caitlin turned. It was a tall, self-assured man in a suit. A carnation stood at dapper attention in his breast pocket. He looked familiar, but she couldn't say from where. He seemed out of place there in the baby furniture store, so bizarre with his flower and overly formal suit. 'You look familiar . . .' she said. Then he smiled and that triggered something: 'The cab, that day, your cab. You jump-started my jeep. That's it, isn't it?' She clenched her hand triumphantly and snapped her finger.

The man laughed. An easy laugh. 'I do remember too. You were shopping for toys that day, I believe.' He turned to face her more fully. 'You were shopping for toys, weren't you?'

'Yes.'

'And you know what else? I think you were at the birthing class I attended once.'

'At the Holbrook Center?'

'The very place!'

'That's nice of you to attend. More fathers should. But not many do,' she said. He laughed again. The laugh came easy, but with stage-like ease. She was reminded of watching a game show host or a soap opera actor in the dusk of his career. But he was very polished, very smooth. She couldn't quite place him from the birthing class. But she never was very attentive there, and she'd stopped going since the tragedy. 'Have you gone lately? I don't know if you heard about Claudia? You may have read in the papers . . .'

'No, I don't follow the news.' He adjusted his carnation and looked Caitlin in the eye. 'And I didn't know any Claudia. What happened?'

'A small woman, very pregnant, very kind. She was brutally attacked and murdered in the Holbrook parking lot. They say she was butchered. That her baby was . . .' Caitlin's voice gave a little, and she decided not to continue. She hadn't really known Claudia either, but there was a camaraderie among the regulars at the birthing group. Caitlin had cried for hours when she'd heard about the assault. She'd cried even more upon imagining the never-to-be-born baby ripped from the womb. It reeked of politics and theology to decide for herself whether the 'it' had been a young person or only a biological precursor. But Caitlin still grieved for a young soul that had never been realised. And she recoiled at the terror of the gruesome crime.

'That's a tragedy, all right.' The man seemed lost in thought but unaffected, hearing the news as if it was the Dow Jones ticker on a slow trading day. But then a sadness came into his eyes.

Caitlin looked at the strange man – with the carnation, the suddenly sympathetic eyes, and the suit that she now noticed was more than a little threadbare. He was very unusual for a cab driver, whatever that meant. 'When is your wife expecting?'

'Huh?' He seemed lost in thought now. 'Ah – expecting.' The sympathetic eyes disappeared and the stage demeanour took its place. 'Well, we're not married,' he said with precision. 'She's expecting in one month, though.' He looked at his watch as if that would provide the exact time. 'One month.'

They both turned to look at the crib.

'Me too, one month.'

'She's very excited.'

'I'm excited, but scared.'

'She's scared too.'

'I'm delighted. I've dreamed this.'

'She's delighted. It's also her dream.'

'There was an infertility problem at first. His sperm, well...'

'That also sounds familiar,' he said in a very tender, wistful tone.

Caitlin paused to admire his candour. Of course, she had also spoken with honesty. But to hear a man speak so openly about his own problems like that. It impressed her. She couldn't possibly imagine Paul having the same conversation.

She looked about the great space of the store. A salesman ambled down an aisle; a cash register somewhere was printing up a receipt; another child was trying his hand at the gumball machine. The man pointed at her belly. 'That's something similar, right there.'

Caitlin looked down and considered herself as if he'd pointed to a ketchup stain on her dress. It occurred to her that one pregnancy *was* much like the next – an easily recognisable phenomenon with certain standard characteristics. But to the parents themselves, there was very little about one that resembled the other. A pregnancy was clinical and similar until it was yours. Then it became an absolutely unique element, with physical properties all its own.

'I'm not sure the mother would agree,' Caitlin said with a smile.

'Well, that's an interesting question.'

'It's kind of you to take on all this work – shopping for the crib, and all that.'

'This kind of thing I enjoy. You know, to plan for the little one. To get all the bric-à-brac that I can afford. What could be more fun? I really can't wait. I'm on tenterhooks as it is. And then every purchase, it gets me one small step closer.' He pinched his fingers in a gesture of tininess.

'I know what you mean. I feel as though I might faint a million times a day. I'm ready, though. I've never been so excited, but I'm ready.'

'I see it as a precious gift. I assume you feel the same way.'

'Yes,' said Caitlin dreamily.

'That's why the horror of a baby being ripped from the womb like that. It makes me ill. Sickening,' he said.

'Yes.'

'By the way, you really do remind me of her.'

'Of who?'

'Of the mother of my baby.'

'Oh.'

They were both turned towards the crib again looking down, and Caitlin was reminded of newlyweds gazing over the falls at Niagara. And as if she were really there, looking into that chasm of explosive surf, she felt the unpleasant tug of vertigo grip her.

She hadn't mentioned what happened to Claudia a moment ago – or had she? She hadn't mentioned the butchery, the brutality, or what had happened to the baby.

Ripped from the womb.

Or had she?

Now she couldn't even be sure. She tried to think. But it was too exhausting. Obviously she *had* mentioned it. He knew. How else would he know? It was in all the papers.

But he'd said he didn't read the papers, hadn't he? She felt herself drifting, dizzy – the vertigo. She felt as though she might faint. She was feeling that way more and more recently. She had an image of an elevator door closing, on Claudia's face, as though in a nightmare. And a face beside hers that she didn't recognise. But she *had* told him. Now she remembered. She *had* told him. She *must have*. Yes, *she had*.

'Are you all right?' He was staring at her, with an earnest look of concern. 'You look pale.'

She felt the blood returning along with her strength. 'Yes, I'm fine. I had a brief dizzy spell. I'd better go. This pregnancy stuff, you know. It's all new to me.'

'Well, it was nice seeing you.'

'Yes.'

'You really do remind me of her . . .' he said with an unbalanced grin. But she didn't see him or hear him. She was already out the door. As she left, he was inside next to the gumball machine, watching her. He was watching with a statue-like stillness, as if he'd already been watching for a long, long while.

MISBEGOTTEN

31

Chemistry was such a part of life, thought Crapshoot as he pistol-whipped the bearded, middle-aged man and tossed him on to the sidewalk. Take the fingerprints, for example, that could have been dusted and rendered damning had he not worn disposable surgical gloves and taken the added precaution of wrapping each of his fingertips in Scotch tape. Take the blood that now coated the black Mercedes leather and would be removed with a special cleanser designed not to damage the finish. Take the revolutionary quick-drying paint that even as he thought about it was being applied to the car and turning the car from silver to green. Take the semen he'd donated.

Ten minutes later he emerged on Barrow Street to hear the sirens and see the squad cars speeding around the corner. He glanced down to double-check his suit: *spotless. Now that was the way.* He removed the Scotch tape pieces from his fingertips one by one and dropped them down a gutter grate. A slow drizzle began and he decided to get some food.

In the Dunkin' Donuts, all was quiet. The news hadn't arrived yet. Reg was asleep and the counterboy was mopping up some coffee from the dirty tile floor.

'Where's Marty?'

'Not in, it's past noon,' answered the counterboy, stooping to pull an unidentifiable piece of coffee-soaked refuse from the mop tentacles.

'Did you hear the sirens? Must be another carjack.'

'Didn't hear them.'

The counterboy always lied. Crapshoot knew Marty was in back studying the racing odds and that the sirens had been so loud they'd almost woken up Reg. Crapshoot had an impulse to pummel the counterboy against the donut case, to bloody another face mercilessly as he'd done only minutes earlier outside, but he was never a man to act on impulse and instead he stepped slowly behind the counter to help himself to coffee and a donut.

The coffee in hand and a warm donut nestled in a bag at his hip, he started up his cab and headed for Westbridge. He was plotting his own chemistry experiment. Like a mischievous young science student who has just discovered that you can create a small explosion with a few simple household ingredients, he chuckled at the thrill of it. Crapshoot realised, when he'd watched her through the harsh sunlight of that afternoon in the parking lot, that he owned a part of her; and when he'd talked to her at the furniture store, that his ownership was growing with each passing day. And that Caitlin Bourke, as she sat in the security of her Range Rover and her purchases, had no idea of his ownership. Then as now, the discovery titillated him and he felt the gnawing in his chest that signalled his excitement.

He remembered the words dripping slowly from the pen, the right line for the card on her baby shower present. He was not concerned with art – or feelings – but with result. He wanted words which would amplify her loneliness as she sat in those many rooms and contemplated his child.

MISBEGOTTEN

And it was *his* child.

His child.

Crapshoot had never had a child and was unfamiliar with how that might feel, but he was certain that whenever there was something that was potentially *his*, he'd struggled to guard it like a pitbull around a marrowbone.

The roads to Westbridge reminded him of a wet ribbon. And ribbons reminded him of the beautifully wrapped present that sat quietly in the trunk. He'd thought long and hard about a proper gift for Caitlin's shower. The type of thing that the Toy Park sold was too pedestrian for his tastes. *A Barbie doll . . . a Ken doll.* Yes, they could make the average child happy. But this was *his* child, and the mother of *his* child. Surely he would have to provide something extraordinary – something that would be remembered. He would never stand to be a father that did less than leave his mark in the world. It was hard, though, to imagine the right gift for anyone, let alone Caitlin. Crapshoot had always felt cash was the best present: liquid currency to allow maximum freedom. Who really wanted all that clothing that didn't fit? Those ugly trinkets that ended up at the next yard sale? The mail-order catalogue item that went back the next day?

It was safer to send cash. Everyone appreciated it. But cash wasn't unique. One hundred-dollar bill looked much like the rest. It would be forgotten when the last penny rolled away. To leave an impression, you had to leave a memento, something with memory. Memories – at least as long as they were memories – did not roll away.

The inspiration had come to him when he'd watched a throng of children playing with abandon outside a school. They were so sure of their own bodies, blessed with a lack of any knowledge of their fragility, swinging this way and that as they clambered to the top of the jungle gym and jumped down again. Crapshoot had pictured those young bodies, unformed, in the womb, struggling for nourishment and clambering, even then, for a leg up.

And then, weeks later, on that particular night, he'd known what to get Caitlin.

The Bourke house had a few lights on and he saw the strange cars in the driveway parked placidly next to the Range Rover. He sat in the darkness of his cab and dribbled a slight amount of spittle on to his glazed donut. Were he to watch under a magnifying glass he would see an actual chain reaction at work: the catalysing enzymes of saliva breaking down the carbohydrates, lowering the needed effort of natural processes of disintegration. That's what was beautiful about catalysts, thought Crapshoot. They only made life a little easier. The rest was left to nature. So much of science was actually not artificial – just an aiding and abetting of the purely natural. So little effort, such far-flung results. A well-wrought experiment, like a bit of spittle, so simple and so natural: enough to pierce the brain and unravel it.

He went around back to the trunk and opened it to retrieve the package. It was elegantly wrapped. Yellow and blue and purple ribbons were pulled tautly around the sides only to cascade in dazzling splendour from the top. The wrapping paper itself was festive and bright, with geometric shapes in cheerfully recurring patterns. Crapshoot looked at it admiringly. He waited.

He was not used to gift-giving. He had to admit the old homily was accurate: it *was* a good feeling to give instead of always to get.

32

'There's something else for you out here, Caitlin!' Jackie was smiling at the front door, white caps, flushed cheeks, dyed blonde hair. Jackie Jergens was heir to an industrial fortune and social czarina of Clinton Oaks, the most exclusive knot of Westbridge real estate. 'It's beautifully wrapped. It must be dull. The most boring presents always come in the best packages.'

Caitlin stayed on the living-room couch. It wasn't what she wanted to do now: open yet another present. Despite, or maybe because of, the thrill of ripping off a hundred ribbons, she was exhausted and didn't want to deal with another well-meaning present until Christmas.

'Could you do me a favour and bring it in, Jackie?'

'Sure, darling.' Jackie came in holding a magnificently wrapped box. The exhaustion came again and Caitlin allowed herself to melt back into the couch. Jackie was tilting the box back and forth, trying to guess the contents. 'I'll put it here on the mantel. It's a showpiece of a wrapping job if I ever saw one. Maybe it's from Reynold's. I wouldn't even open it. Just let it sit there and look pretty. Boy what a baby paradise this is just about now. Everything ready to go.' A look of panic whipped her head around. 'Not that *you're* ready to go,

Caitlin. One thing you don't want to do is go into labour early.'

It was a tiring day. Caitlin had never thought receiving so many gifts would have been such a chore. A litter of different papers and bows and packing materials surrounded her like the debris after a riot. Baby boy clothes of every description sat and waited impatiently to be put to use. Nearly everything was a large size, designed for a four-year-old. They'd all avoided small newborn-sized items, thinking someone else would get those. As it was, the cascade of overalls and dungarees and turtlenecks lounged about like the disembodied fashions of another generation.

Serena came in from the kitchen, holding an empty whiskey glass to one eye like a monocle. 'Damn, it's stuffy in here, Caitlin. It must be all that hot air of a gaggle of girls gossiping and gift-giving. Makes me sick. That's why I didn't get you anything.'

'I wouldn't want you to put yourself out,' said Caitlin. It was true that there was something vacuous and demeaning about a baby shower. It was archaic to have a bunch of women get together and exchange powder-blue gifts while their husbands were out golfing. But it was part of the routine of birth in a town like this, no less expected than regular doctor visits and good wishes from the neighbours.

'I remember when Melanie gave birth early and it was in the incubator for two months,' Jackie continued, oblivious to any conversation around her. 'She couldn't even hold it. The poor dear was about three pounds. My God, three pounds is exactly what I need to lose. And to think! That's all this little one had! It makes you cry. But God does provide. Oh let's open this present, OK Caitlin? One more gift for the road. I'll open it?'

Caitlin nodded.

'You guys take your gift for the road. I'll take the

proverbial drink instead,' said Serena, disappearing again into the kitchen.

'So the father's a poet,' said Jackie, lowering her voice confidentially. 'Serena told me,' she added in answer to the expected question. 'But don't worry. I won't tell anyone.' She sat on the couch opening the last present, unravelling the paper and folding it carefully as if she were going to save it for the next holiday. That way of opening presents had always bothered Caitlin. Presents were supposed to be spontaneous and fun. Not so deliberate. No wonder Jackie found the best-wrapped presents so dull. She was too busy unwrapping them.

She thought of saying 'Please *do* keep it to yourself, Jackie' but the idea of Jackie keeping a secret was even more absurd than folding used wrapping paper into neat little squares.

The comment did trigger her to think of what *he* was doing then: perhaps writing furiously or considering passionately, with shoulders hunched over a humble kitchen table or with feet regally propped on an ottoman. The idea that he was creating poetry as she was creating his child heartened her. And the idea that his life work was taking place in a different world than her own, separate from society functions and insignificant gifts, made her emotions dilate. Regions in her consciousness were aware that he was out there, thinking in some way about her and their child. Caitlin thought of the future: a cold grey morning on an autumn day, tea steeping in the kitchen, a baby in the high chair. And the silence of the house not so loud any more.

'Unbelievable!' exclaimed Jackie.

'What?' asked Caitlin.

'If it's not another pair of overalls,' she said, taking them out of the box and placing them in front of Caitlin. 'What did I tell you, darling? The best box: the most boring presents. And it's from ...' she hesitated, pulling the notecard from amongst the piles of tissue paper. '... George and Ellen Glover. What a couple of two-faced phonies they are. You know right now they're bad-mouthing the both of us.'

'Right. At least we *never* do that.'

A drunken call of 'Touché' drifted in from the kitchen. The sun was setting and long shadows were cast on the far wall.

'Do you want us to stay a bit, Caitlin? Night's falling.'

'Thanks, but that's fine, Jackie. I'm a big girl now.'

By the time the full dark arrived, Jackie and Serena had left and Caitlin was alone waiting for Paul to come home from his dinner at the club. The waiting had soothed her as the dusk drifted down into the windows and brought with it the calm that allowed her to rest. The darkness had come swiftly and the calm had become lonely. It was times like this that the thought of what was inside her saved her. But there were still doubts. The dizziness sometimes worried her. Morning sickness was expected at the beginning but why *now*? Yet the worry was nothing next to the happiness. No one could take away her baby. It was part of her.

She toured the house gingerly and decided that she would deal with the mess the next day. A million crickets were singing in the dark outside. She pressed her face against the glass of the large sliding door in the living room. It was like a one-way mirror: to look into a suburban night like this was to see nothing except herself. With the lights of the house ablaze, there was no way to probe the darkness of the woods. Whatever was out there was invisible. When they had first moved into the house this had terrified her. She'd immediately ordered thick shades to cover up what must appear like a display case of department store furnishings from the outside. Paul had ordered a few spotlights to illuminate the surrounding grounds but they only reached the limited areas of the doors and the driveway. And then only a few yards. The dark was deep and impenetrable. It wasn't the reality of burglars or stalkers but fears much more primal and unpronounceable that called to her. A suburban house in six acres of woods like these was very much alone at night. She recalled a friend telling her that all a criminal had to do was cut the phone wires and jam the alarm and then the house would be as alone as a frontier cabin.

Thinking these thoughts, she jumped when the doorbell rang.

For Paul to forget his keys was surprising so she asked who it was, telling herself the fear was ridiculous. She fixed the security chain under the lock.

'It's me, Billy, the cab driver – the father from the birthing class. I just brought you a gift for your shower. A little belated I know – '

She opened the door four inches so that the chain was taut. She peered past the frame and into his eyes: the same suit, neatly pressed; the carnation, a bit wilted; the eyes, friendly now. There was a large, nicely wrapped gift in his hands.

'That's kind of you.'

He waited a polite moment. 'Do you mind opening the door?' And: 'I heard about the shower from Alexa. She gave me the address. Nice woman. I told her I wanted to surprise you. Sorry I'm so late. Won't you let me in?' It was awkward to hold a neighbour outside like that, but she'd never opened the door for anyone after dark. Like the firmest of the ten commandments, the edict against opening a door to a stranger at night weighed heavily on her heart. 'I know it's late, but I'm no stranger,' he said with his broad smile. 'After all, we birthing class members have to stick together.' He laughed unconvincingly.

Was it the hollow laugh then that triggered it?

She saw him through the open four inches of the door and his head was framed like a thin religious icon. And then she had a flash of memory: to an elevator door closing that night on Claudia and a single other face next to hers – his face, thinly framed then, as it was now. It was in that extra, slow second that she saw his face as if for the first time. She saw pupils dilate, the mouth fall into a frown.

'I don't want to upset you. You're right to be cautious. Think of what can happen alone in these woods after dark. No one would even hear a scream that carried a mile – very much like in that parking lot the night of the birthing class. I'll just leave this present for you here and go.' She didn't answer, but only watched him stoop and let the package slip to the flagstone patio. She was frozen, unable even to close the door, waiting for him to turn and leave. A moment became an hour. She found herself listening for Paul's car but there was only the sound of the crickets. He got up, straightened his jacket sleeves and straightened his carnation. 'Really, I'll be going now. You'll appreciate the gift.' And then he added: 'Claudia would have appreciated it.' He smiled. And she saw, clearly, that the smile was sickly. 'You'll see that we know each other better than you think we do. You should've let me in.' She felt herself begin to utter the word *why* and then it drowned somewhere within her.

With that he walked briskly off the patio, down the drive and into the night.

And she knew before she opened the box that she would open it.

And she knew what she would find.

33

He sat in the curtain of woods by the house and waited for the scream. He was used to waiting by now, but he wouldn't have to wait long: maybe a second or two. He looked back and saw the lights of the house, dancing with bright merriment like a freshly adorned Christmas tree, and the shadowy, pregnant figure on the patio.

He was reminded of waiting for a car to turn on to Morone. There was the same sense of power and the chase. He waited as he did then: he had laid the trap, he had performed his cruelty – he was merely waiting for it all to take effect.

His experiment.

When the first scream pierced the night even beyond his own predictions, he nodded his head with understanding. It was like pouring acid on the largest wound. And then there was a second scream more hideous than the first: curdling, lingering, possessed by the horror he'd cultivated.

He walked to his cab with the help of his penlight and started on the long way home.

34

There were voices, but she didn't want to hear them. Hearing them only signalled having to return to them. She buried her head into the pillow, trying to stave off memory. But there the voices didn't go away. She heard Paul's again. Reassuring, calming – earnest.

There, there, sleep a little more.

She knew she had to be strong. They were all waiting for her to be strong. She was waiting for herself to be strong. Maybe a little more Valium was what she needed instead.

There, there, just go back to sleep.

She felt Paul's hand, soothing on her forearm, a man's touch. She saw Serena standing in the background and then moving closer. Serena took her other hand and smiled.

Go on, baby doll, get some sleep for Mama Serena.

She looked down at her stomach and remembered.

She screamed.

'Relax, honey. Relax and sleep. The baby's fine. Dr Lynch gave you a clean bill of health and Dr Dotterweich will be here shortly. And the baby's fine. You're doing fine, honey, you're doing fine.'

She couldn't make out the other voices. She looked

through the room and out into the hall. There was the blue of a policeman. There were suits. Too many people. She saw them pass by the frame of the bedroom door. And memory started to pull her in again: a face within a frame, the elevator closing, Claudia's face, and *his* – then she stopped. Blackness came to protect her from going further.

Dotterweich stared at the Bourke home. It was large and comfortable like many clients' homes. A fine place to raise a child. In the surrounding dark, it was startlingly bright. The house looked normal and serene, except for the police cruisers parked in front.

He'd foreseen some type of problem with the Bourkes. He knew something would not gel. It had been impossible for him to describe it, but he'd known. There was always the risk that when you tried to trick evolution, you would incur the wrath of all biology.

Biology.

Not mother nature. Not God. No witches stood brewing eyes of newt and casting spells. Science was more subtle. Evolution was masterful in its complexity and beauty. But to tame it, you ran the risks. Biology knew more about itself than anyone. Chromosomes were programmed for a purpose. They would not be fooled. There were risks.

'Dr Dotterweich?' The man flashed a badge. He was a pockmarked police lieutenant in plain clothes.

'Yes, I'm Dotterweich.' He bowed slightly with European servility.

'Mrs Bourke is resting in the bedroom upstairs.' He shrugged towards the long staircase. 'I'd like to ask you some quick questions first.'

'I'll be more than happy to help you, sir. *After* I attend to my patient.'

MISBEGOTTEN

The lieutenant waved him upstairs. 'As you like. I'll be waiting for you here.'

In the bedroom, Paul Bourke was diligently attending to his wife, stroking her hand again and again. A woman with frizzy hair and a suspicious gaze sat on a wicker ottoman in the corner.

Paul turned. 'Hello, Doctor. It's good to see you. She's sleeping now.'

'Good. Sleep is best.'

'Our internist came earlier. He said the baby's fine. Thank God that – '

Dotterweich put out his thick palm. 'Let's not discuss it. I will check the baby myself. The baby *will* be fine. Now, if you'll both excuse me, I'm going to visit with Mrs Bourke for a few minutes, alone.' He sat down at the bedside and put his fingers on Caitlin's wrist to check her pulse while he waited for the others to leave. When the door shut, he asked:

'Mrs Bourke, how are you?'

The eyelids flickered, then opened. 'I'm OK, Dr Dotterweich.'

'I know you are. You look healthy and strong,' he lied. 'The baby will be fine. You've just had a bad fright. I heard all about it on the phone from Paul. You don't have to talk about it. This sick individual will be apprehended by the police. So you need not worry. I'm told that the police know who he is. Some type of professional felon from Northport.'

'What you heard is not all.'

'Oh?'

Caitlin started to cough; her face grew still more pale.

'Relax. Whatever it is, we can handle it.'

She reached under the blanket. 'This – ' she held out a small notecard – 'was attached to *it*. I hid this card from the police, I hid it from Paul. I'd hide it from myself if I could.'

He took the note and read the three short words:

For poetry's sake.

As he read them, he knew he would remember the moment for ever. It was one of those moments when the force of realisation, so indelible, leaves no doubt that what has been witnessed will be retained.

He had always taught himself to guard against emotion, to remember the tenets of science and reason. Life was too complex to do otherwise. But human sickness had always intervened. The human condition was such that true deviance did not fit into the evolutionary pattern. He had often wondered about the nature of deviance and what role it played in biology's plan. He had not yet found a satisfactory answer.

'I see,' he replied simply. He remembered that phrase quite well. He remembered the very handwriting on the application. He remembered Caitlin's concerns about the letters she had received – concerns he had put no stock in. 'I'm sorry.'

He could not think for a moment of what else to say. 'There must be some mistake ...' he started, without conviction. But the words sounded too hollow.

Caitlin sat up in bed. She was strong and firm. Her voice quavered but it was steady in its meaning: 'I must know if he's the father. If he *is*, I must have an immediate abortion.'

He found himself responding as if by rote, 'You're in the final month, Mrs Bourke. The legality of – '

'I don't give a damn about what's legal and what's not.' She sat up on her elbows, eyes pink, lip quivering with anger. 'Your quack clinic is what's illegal. Your sick preaching is what's illegal. Your silly convictions, your crackpot lectures, your – ' But her fury was expended. She sank back into the pillow and sighed.

'Please, Mrs Bourke, lie back and try to relax. I do understand the grave pain in this. I will resolve the situation. I can do some paternity tests against Paul to see if he's, well, the father, and then . . . Hopefully. Hopefully this, this beast, is not and . . .' He found his fluency with words waning. 'Time is short, though. The baby could come along any minute – frankly.'

Caitlin sat there, silent, watching him. He abandoned himself to her reproach and nodded. She had every right to hate him until the end of time. But he did not know whether to fault himself or biology. Or some other fixture of the human condition. There was always the possibility of a donor not being what they presented in a fertility application. But to imagine such a horror as this: a psychopath wanting to pass on his seed and then torment the helpless. It was anathema to all he'd learned. The very foundation of his beliefs was cracking slowly within his silence. It was as though he had depended for too long on the purely biological. The pathological he'd ignored.

'I don't blame you,' she said finally.

'You have every right to blame me. I take full responsibility, legal, moral and otherwise. I say that now, on the record, and I'll say it again at any point you ask.'

'Please, I don't blame you. I can't blame you and I'm too tired to blame myself. I'm weary of all emotion. I would blame the heavens if I had faith. But since I lack even that I just want to be strong. I just want to know if he's the father. That is all I need to know. If he's the father, then I must destroy it. If Paul's the father, then I will keep it.'

'You can blame whoever will absorb the blame. And in this case that might as well be me. That is healthier than any other course. We will handle this situation. Will you tell the police or should I?'

'I'll tell Paul first. And then I'll tell the police.'

He shook his head sadly. 'Life is not for the meek, not this life nor any other. Thankfully, you're not meek, Mrs Bourke.'

'Sometimes, Dr Dotterweich, you talk more like a priest than a doctor.'

'I have always put little stock in religion. But who can deny that there are times when a little faith would be useful.'

'Let me know . . .'

'I will. Now sleep.'

He turned to make his exit. There was something about leaving that room that reminded him of leaving a wake and he did feel very much like a priest just then. There were times when the roles of doctor and priest were necessarily fused. This was such a time. He encountered the pockmarked police officer downstairs.

'You ready?' the policeman asked.

'Yes.'

'You heard about the suspect who butchered the foetus and brought it here? A known criminal who operates out of the Northport area.'

'I heard.'

'Right. What's the link, Doctor?'

'What's the link?'

'Between Mrs Bourke and the suspect.' The policeman stared at him. Police had a way of staring. They stared from a calculated angle as if they could pry the truth from between the cornea and the iris. In his native country he'd learned to spend as little time as possible with the police.

MISBEGOTTEN

And in America, he'd learned nothing to the contrary. But he was not even trying to hide the truth. Still the stare was relentless. 'You handled the artificial insemination of Mrs Bourke, did you not?'

'I did.'

'And that went smoothly?'

'It did.'

'And the donor is?'

'Mrs Bourke will tell you that as soon as she tells her husband.' Dotterweich looked at Paul Bourke wandering aimlessly about the living room searching for a task. He felt pity and a type of scorn for Mr Bourke: he knew so little of his wife. And now he would have to learn a horror of horrors.

The path to his car was dark and Dotterweich stumbled once. The dark was menacing. He allowed himself to imagine the scene of a few hours earlier – when a lonely Caitlin Bourke stood and received a cruel delivery. He shuddered at the thought. It was harrowing to see the illness of humanity. Despite its many strides, evolution was always taking one step backward. Backward into a night as deep as the one he walked through.

Caitlin Bourke sat in bed and waited for dawn. Paul would come up soon. Most of the police would leave. One cruiser would stay to protect them until the arrest was made. It all sat below her like theatre on the grand stage – all the activity and she no longer a character. She longed for yesterday when hope had guarded her. She looked down at her belly but didn't allow herself to speculate on the possibilities. Slowly panic would build within her until she felt the urge to scream, but then she remembered she had to be strong.

She should be able to sense who the father was. Surely

a mother must be able to tell. Surely all of Dotterweich's theories would say so. Before there were paternity tests, mothers could sense it. Just as before calculators, people could add. And before faxes, people could wait a day. She would have to know. She said a prayer to know and fell asleep, part of her hoping never to wake again.

35

'The rent, Billy.' The dispatcher raised his arm, then thought better of it.

Crapshoot had such disdain for the dispatcher's coarse ways. Crapshoot dropped the two twenties and headed for the door.

'Billy, you got to like me more than forty this month. Rent's going up. You know how things are.' The dispatcher opened his Chinese food and stuck half an egg roll in his mouth.

'What's wrong? Chess game not going well these days?' Crapshoot inquired.

'Oh no. My game's OK. It's your game that needs a little fixin'.'

'Oh?'

'Cops came by today. They asked me a few questions. They wanted to know if you still worked here, where they could find you. I didn't let it worry me. Until they asked about you and some dead girl. Then I started talking baseball – you know – to change the subject. They didn't like that. And you know what, Billy, I got bored of talking baseball myself. Next time they come by, I might have to talk about what they want to talk about.' The dispatcher smiled. A strand of pork fat hung tentatively from his teeth.

Extortion.

Now that was sophisticated for the dispatcher, a man who Crapshoot had figured to be content to collect his petty rent and cab fares like an overfed, complacent burgher on a slow Sunday afternoon. This sudden quirk in his method was deserving of respect. Perhaps the dispatcher was a true chess player, a man of the world, of many moves, with red queens up his soiled sleeves, and a trick rook hidden in his girth.

Crapshoot, as would any businessman, quickly came to a well-considered decision.

'You can talk about baseball or cricket or even chess. Or you can talk about me. But if you talk about me, then your chess-playing days are over. You've heard of checkmate? Once I've sliced your throat, I'll use your stubby pinkies as pawns and your stubbier toes as bishops. And then that squat pod you call a penis ... It's your choice.' The dispatcher looked nervous, but not at the threat. He was looking out of the corner of his eye. Something was up.

Crapshoot turned on his leather heel and pretended to go back to his desk. Then he slipped off to the closet behind the watercooler and lifted the trapdoor to the cellar. He let himself down into the cool, dusty space and hustled along the narrow passageway. And not a second too soon. The shouts of policemen filled the room upstairs. So the dispatcher was really a player after all. He'd set him up. But Crapshoot had been too quick. All great things come to this, he thought, the adrenalin shooting through his groin like a hypodermic hit.

I am always in season.

He hadn't thought the police would peg him so soon. Now he'd have to go undercover earlier than he'd expected. But he was well prepared. He ran along the passageway, stripping down to his undershirt and pants and shoving the other clothes into an open pipe. He tossed the holster and kept the gun in his hand. A disguise would come later. Such was his dapper reputation on the street that a disguise was relatively easy.

At the end of the corridor he knocked out the wood slats and stepped up into a back alley. He sprinted down the alley to an abandoned garbage pile. He stood atop the pile and then descended to Acorn Street. A quick walk up the block and he saw two unmarkeds sitting in front of the taxi stand. That meant they had at least six men undercover watching the front. By now they'd discovered the trapdoor. But not him.

He headed for Macroy's to pick up a car. He would need to clear out of town and make his moves. The game would have to go on. This was the biggest game he'd ever played and you didn't fold the hand when you were still holding the red queen.

He stopped at a pay phone off the Merritt and placed the call. She answered on the third ring.

36

One ring. Two rings . . . Caitlin knew it was him.

'Hello?' she said, trying to keep her voice contained.

'Don't hang up,' came the gravelly voice. She immediately felt the nausea. If he called, she had to talk to him, the police said. She had to hold him on the line – at least two minutes – long enough for the tap. Paul sat on the couch opposite, staring at the floor. He'd been staring at the floor since he'd been told. His head still hung in his hands, next to his fourth whiskey on the coffee table. He occasionally rotated his eyes upward and looked at her womb as if he'd never seen it before. And perhaps he hadn't really. Caitlin looked outside at the cruiser sitting in the driveway. It made her feel a little safer.

'The police can't help you,' he said.

So he must be watching, somehow, even then. From within her womb he must be watching, from within her very soul. She retched.

His voice continued, steady and cruel: 'I composed a new poem for you. After all, you are the mother of my child. I've committed the lines to memory. They're not so good. But they rhyme and they're to the point. I think you'll enjoy them. Do you mind if I read it?'

She didn't respond. Her voice wouldn't come.

'OK then. I'll begin:

What's that thumping you feel at night?
It's me, in your womb, the dark inside the light.
What's your possibility for escape?
None. I live within you – a test tube rape.'

She started to cry, the tears she'd promised herself not to give him came anyway. She cried as Paul moaned softly in the corner. But *he* was not deterred by the crying, his voice amplified in its maudlin crooning over the police tape recorder:

'I plumbed your being with an identity fake
Your baby, now mine, for poetry's – '

But she slammed down the receiver. She refused to hear that last familiar rhyme.
   The pain would not relent. She couldn't look down at herself, touch the shape of her belly, without feeling a tremendous revulsion at what resided within her – and guilt at her own feelings.
   She rose from the couch. It was not easy to get up now with the pregnancy so advanced. She scaled the stairs unsteadily, blind to her own movements. In the bedroom she found herself stumbling through the dark, over towels, and around the bed and to the closet. She sat on the carpeting at the foot of the closet and wept for a minute. Then she reached up and took down a wire hanger. She pulled up her maternity dress and felt inside her underwear. Life was very fragile, she thought, imagining herself straightening the hanger's curve, then starting to thread the cold metal inside her. She imagined pushing up, a little higher. Pain came and she winced but did not feel. A

little higher. She imagined drawing blood. But the wrong kind. She was only hurting herself. She imagined pushing deeper and deeper. The cold metal within her: it was almost soothing.

She felt a hand on her shoulder. 'What are you doing?' asked Paul, taking the hanger from her hand. 'Why don't you lie down on the bed?' She gladly submitted to the warm sheets. Paul came over and stroked her forehead kindly. After a moment, he said: 'I understand how hard it is.'

'I want to kill *myself*. Not the baby.'

'I know.'

She knew that Paul kept a loaded gun in his bedside table drawer, under a knit scarf. She fantasised about using it later, when the house was quiet again. She wished Paul would leave her alone, so she could use it. It became a recurring image in her mind: the gun in her mouth, the shot – then nothing, relief from life. But what if she failed to do a proper job?

'I'll sleep now,' she said.

'Good.' He went to the bathroom and ran the water while she watched shadows dance on the ceiling with glazed eyes. He came back and lay on the bed next to her.

'There was a time, not long ago, when I hoped it wasn't your child.'

'Yes, I know,' he said quietly.

'You know?'

'I understand too.'

She saw in the shadows her fate. 'He'll return, you know. He'll come for his child. I sense it.' An idea spawned in her head.

'Don't,' he said, putting his hand over her mouth. 'He won't ever come here again.'

'No,' she said. 'He'll come.' And she knew, as sure as she knew that the movements in her belly signified another being, that she was right.

MISBEGOTTEN

37

The ribbon of the road sang to him.

He was high with his mission. The air blasted through the windows and Crapshoot stared straight ahead, hands clenching the wheel, looking forward to the moment when he would hit the Westbridge exit. It would take just over three minutes from the first stop light. By now, he'd timed the route many times and could map the way by heart. He knew to expect police. In knowing that, he knew what to do. Never had he experienced the police as any more than a minor challenge.

I am always in season.

The exit came. He eased the car to a stop and listened to the trees: it was quiet at this hour and still black. There was the sound of the crickets but not much else. He remembered the piercing screams of that night and felt the gnawing in his heart. He drove on, into the Westbridge early morning.

38

The gun rested on her lap.

She sat on the couch in the living room with the gun and waited. She would use it soon. She was waiting for the dawn.

Paul had fallen quickly asleep and she'd come down soon after. She sat, in the very early morning, well used to the dark by now, fingering the gun. Her father had taught her well. She hadn't been a bad shot then. And at a short range, she'd been very good.

She sat and waited.

She hummed a lullaby to herself for a while and then she said to herself, as she had many times already:

If I can shoot when I look him in the eyes, then he can't be the father, because I couldn't possibly shoot the father of my boy. If I can shoot him when I look him in the eyes, then he can't be the father, because I couldn't possibly shoot the father of my boy . . .

This she repeated again and again. It was like a religious incantation – God's word as well as hers. She was certain this would be the test. She released the safety and remembered her father's words on that cold stretch of the shooting range in the years after her mother's death: 'You never take this down until you're ready to fire. Taking off the safety is like having a child. Once you do it, you'd better know what you're doing. And be careful of guns around people. But if you must shoot a man, look him in the eyes when you pull the trigger: you can't shoot a man who has any goodness in his heart when you look him in the eyes.'

If I can shoot when I look him in the eyes, then he can't be the father, because I couldn't possibly shoot the father of my boy. If I can shoot him when I look him in the eyes, then he can't be the father, because I couldn't possibly shoot the father of my boy . . .

Soon, she heard footsteps outside. They were faint, but she knew she'd heard them. She crept by the rear window and dropped to her knees, her swollen belly pressed lightly against the glass. She listened. When he came, she knew he'd come quickly and silently. He would avoid the front of the house where the police cruiser sat. He would come somewhere here, along the sloping rear of the house, where the trees provided fine cover and the spotlights of the house did not reach. She'd thought of explaining that to the police when they'd first arrived, but then she knew that whatever she told them would do no good: he would still find a way.

But she wasn't scared any longer. She was looking forward to the moment of knowing. She wanted him to arrive, to scale the hill in back, to use the cover of the trees, to avoid the harsh spotlights, to trick the police, to break and enter, to come into the living room, to face her and confront her. So that . . .

If I can shoot when I look him in the eyes, then he can't be the father, because I couldn't possibly shoot the father of my boy. If I can shoot him when I look him in the eyes, then he can't be the father, because I couldn't possibly shoot the father of my boy . . .

A queer feeling of elation shot through her and then evaporated like a weak dose of Demerol in the veins. This was the moment when she would know. For better or worse, the suspense would be over. She *would* know. She scanned the darkness for a sign. With the coming dawn, a bit of colour was beginning to show itself between the trees. He would come before sunrise. He would not come by day.

It was always the case, thought Caitlin, that when you were waiting for someone and scoured the horizon to your left, she arrived from the right. If you imagined her wearing a red dress, then she came in black. If you pictured her in a taxi, she showed up on foot. So Caitlin knew as she looked for him down the slope, into the trees, behind the back of the house, that he would arrive via some other path.

Marking her thought was the faint sound of a small glass pane breaking and falling in the kitchen. She knew it was the kitchen because the sound of glass falling on that floor was distinctive. She'd heard it many times. In a nightmarish way, thoughts came to her slowly then. She should have known it would be the kitchen: the kitchen was removed from the lights, from the police, but also from the rapidly rising sun.

You picture them arriving from the left, then they arrive from the right.

Terror came and went. She was left with a cold anxiety. Her hand started to twitch, a small involuntary twitch that she struggled to ignore, while she raised the gun into position with both hands the way her father had taught her. She sat back on the couch, watching the alcove where the living room met the dining room, waiting for him to emerge. Caitlin wondered if Paul was sleeping, and how long he would sleep. She hoped he would sleep. *God, let him sleep through this*, she said under her breath.

He had arrived.

She looked down the barrel of the gun and saw him at

the end of it. He'd walked in softly and now noticed her. She'd pictured him arriving in his pressed suit, a carnation in his pocket, but he was only wearing a T-shirt and pants. He looked a shadow of himself – less imposing except for the long knife he was holding in his right hand.

He smiled. 'I see you were expecting me. Excuse my clothes.' She looked down the barrel of the gun. She couldn't see his eyes but she knew that when he moved a step closer, past the column and into the living room, she would see the whites clearly. She struggled to steady the gun. The twitch would not stop. 'I suggest you put the gun down. You know you won't use it,' he said.

If I can shoot when I look him in the eyes, then he can't be the father, because I couldn't possibly shoot the father of my boy.

'Let's face it,' he continued. 'You have my property there.' He moved a step closer. 'You may not know this, but *I* am always in season.' He smiled the same sickly smile. He walked another step, into the light.

She was not conscious of the gun firing, but only of her own reaction to it: the vibration throughout her body, the pain in her shoulder, the twitch in her hand finally ceasing.

Epilogue

A baby's cry in the dark, like a gunshot in the suburbs, does not go unnoticed. That peculiar pitch that can rise above all else and grit a parent's teeth is nature's most compelling sound. And to banish it with a pacifier or a smile, or a dry diaper or a bounce on the knee, is the only choice. And then there's the sound of laughter that comes after the soothing, like a symphony on the radio after a roadful of static. And then, afterwards, that particular silence, when the baby sleeps and other sounds return.

These sounds, all of them, were a comfort to Caitlin, and she cherished the screaming as much as the cooing. There were times, at three in the morning, when Paul was sleeping soundly, and she wasn't eager to tend to the baby. But then the feeling that there was *someone* to tend *to* sprouted joyfully within her, and she went with alacrity, true to her mission, down the hall and to a place she was needed. The new house was a blessing to her. She found it warm and inviting. It was smaller than the old one, though it was still in Westbridge. There were many places there where she was needed, especially in the baby's room.

She would stare down at her child, Paul Bourke, Jr, and place a mother's hand on his forehead and thereby comfort his nighttime call. When she looked down at him, and saw the sprightly blue of his outfit, and the more elegant, lively blue of his wet eyes, she knew she was in the best place possible.

He was so compact, a year old, just learning how to walk a bit, with tottering steps that took him one step forward and two steps back. And he was a child now, with devilish looks and mischievous glances and powerful wants that took him way beyond the womb.

There had been worries, when he was still breast-feeding at nine months and he seemed unable to be weaned, so comfortable was he with her nipple, so greedy was he for mammary warmth. Yet, she was eager to please his longings and even indulged them, much to Paul's chagrin, breast-feeding for yet another month and then another. That the suckling was so urgent didn't worry her. To have that other mouth so occupied and so dependent gave her a feeling of wonder.

Caitlin never grew to love Paul as a husband, but she loved him as a father and they both felt the type of closeness that comes with shared horrors. He was called 'deddy' and glowed crimson often with this new-found name, slightly embarrassed by his good fortune and certainly grateful that it was directed to him. Paul was very ready with gifts and clothing of all sorts and was prone to rush off to a store for an impromptu purchase just before coming home from work. Paul's eyes lit up at the moment before gift-giving, slightly nervous at Caitlin's and Paul Jr's reaction and then absolutely pleased with the smiles he received.

Dotterweich kindly sent a birthday card to celebrate Paul Jr's first year on earth:

Just a card to celebrate one year of your biological gift. I wish you and Paul the best of everything. No other parents deserve so much.

The day, not long after the birth, that Dotterweich had called them into the office to disclose the official paternity test results, Paul tapped silently on the steering wheel while driving to the clinic. Caitlin sat in the back, next to the baby seat, comforting Paul Jr and thinking to herself that it did not matter any more: when she looked at the baby she saw someone she loved. Nothing more, nothing less. She could not imagine feeling any other way. There was a change that had occurred in her, with the same suddenness of her conception – a change that signalled a love unqualified.

When Dotterweich said that the results conclusively showed Paul to be the father, the happy tears had fallen freely. In her case it was not so much the relief any more, but the end of the waiting. There had been so much waiting, and then the waiting for the scientific pronouncement: that had been the hardest of all. She had known the answer intuitively since that terrible night, but cold science could always overturn what for her was the instinct of maternity. Caitlin looked at the carpeting in the office and said, *I knew, I knew, I knew,* to herself many times. Then she and Paul hugged quietly before thanking Dotterweich and returning home.

That afternoon they both celebrated with Paul Jr, the three of them huddled in the big bed. They had cuddled and napped and said prayers of thanks. By nightfall, Caitlin walked through the new house and appreciated the way it sounded, full of the murmurs of life.

Caitlin did have nightmares – nightmares that would at first force her to lie awake and stare at the ceiling in a state of fearful paralysis. Sometimes she would go downstairs and call Serena, who was always up having a drink or a good time. But the nightmares gradually became fewer and fewer and finally retreated into the oblivion of normal sleep.

It was the week before the baby's first birthday. Dotterweich was sitting at the desk writing his card. It had always been his custom to write a card to each set of parents on the child's first birthday, to wish them good luck for the future.

With the Bourkes, the writing of the card held special importance, but he didn't know the words that could properly convey his feelings. He settled for the usual platitudes and placed the card into the out box to be mailed the next day. His final piece of correspondence.

In his office, boxes were piled against the wall, records waiting to be removed and burned. The records of names and identities, donors and recipients, numbers and addresses, would at last find true anonymity. Outside his window, the world looked unkind. He watched the wind whip up the tree limbs and then die down, its anger spent. Nature was so defective. He dreamed one day of a perfect natural equilibrium, with each creature living and dying in health and fulfilment, and each offspring a gift and a promise.

Some day, he whispered to himself.

Dotterweich fingered the tray on the desk where, months ago, he'd burned the paternity test result. When he discovered that Paul wasn't the father, he knew he could never tell Caitlin. She thought she knew and in those thoughts she was content. To her, intuition *was* knowing. A while ago, the lack of science in her thought process would have disturbed him. Now he was grateful for the human spirit that gave her strength. He refused to be the one to disturb her happiness. Happiness was more important than the biological, he'd learned. And Caitlin and Paul had found happiness. With happiness he dared not tamper.

It was not out of any concern for his own fate or reputation that he lied to her. He was giving up the fertility business anyway. Not selling it. Just abandoning it. He had lost the faith. For him faith was a strange word anyway. Faith was for the religious. But he smiled, thinking about it. Caitlin had told him he talked like a priest. Perhaps it was his eventual calling. He didn't know. He turned out the lights and left the office for the last time.

On a Saturday morning, Caitlin knelt on the carpet of the living-room floor and waited for her baby. He was walking now, still shakily, but with a young resolve that pulled him along. She waited patiently. She could wait for ever. He made a small running burst. He looked to stumble but regained his balance. Then he angled towards his mother, in a sort of freefall. She reached out and grabbed him: to hug him, to catch him, to rescue him. She looked past his smile and into his eyes. They were big and bright. And if they lacked a soul, Caitlin did not know it. It was her baby. Misbegotten, perhaps. But hers.